FROZEN IN FEAR

The Arbuckle Archives:

#1: Deadly Illusion
ISBN: 978-1-77821-631-2

...More coming soon

FROZEN
IN FEAR

ALAN LEBOEUF

FROZEN IN FEAR

Published by Alan LeBoeuf, Edmonton, Canada

ISBN:

Paperback	978-1-77821-632-9
ebook	978-1-77821-635-0

Publication assistance by

PAGEMASTER
PUBLISHING
PageMaster.ca

DEDICATION

Many thanks to all those who have helped me along this journey. Special thanks to Dr. Colleen Braun for comments on the manuscript and to Karen Moffat for the editing. Thanks to those around me who encouraged me to continue when I needed more inspiration than perspiration.

Contents

Meeting your maker
Is never that nice
Especially not, if
You're covered in ice.

CHAPTER 1

"Hello, Lou Diamond Investigations."

"Heh, Sid......Sid.... you there?"

I was there......just. It was eight o'clock on a Sunday morning. I'd had acid indigestion most of the night and hadn't slept a wink. Rita, my future ex, was snoring. Her sleep apnea was playing up, and I had fallen asleep about ten minutes before.

"Louie......what the fuck? Do you know what time it is?"

"Time you get fuck out of bed."

Now I know that line doesn't make sense, but Louie rarely did. He was originally from Romania and had fought a losing battle with the English language since his arrival in Calgary 30 years ago.

It didn't make a lot of sense either at that time of the morning.

But before I go any further, I better tell you who I am. I was born in England but have lived in Calgary for 40 years. I used to be a cop. Enjoyed that, but I never got to my pension. That's another story. I eventually formed a private detective agency. Called it Lou Diamond Investigations. It sounded a bit better than Sid Arbuckle, private dick. I first thought of calling myself Calgary Investigations Associates (CIA). But somebody in the States had stolen that name. Bastards, but I wasn't going to argue. So, it was Lou Diamond Investigations.

Lou Diamond was a guy who'd fucked me over for about 30 grand years before. I think he died about two months later. Thought his name had a bit of panache so I used it. There it was on my business card in gold embossed letters. It worked until I got a call from the tax people. Told me I, Lou Diamond, owed fifteen thousand in back taxes. Told em I wasn't Lou and to bugger off. They never called back.

And Louie? A Calgary cop who kept on the lookout for interesting cases that might make me a bit of money or a bit of a reputation or both. He would probably have gone further in his police career, but when he appeared in court, he was completely incomprehensible.

"What is it, big guy?" I uttered.

"Sid, Sid, ...I've just come across a big stiffy. You should see."

I mean, Louie's sex life was entirely his own business, but I knew that something was being lost in the translation.

"A big stiffy. Yours or somebody else's?" I laughed.

"No, no........a guy has been found just west of Calgary on the Forestry Trunk Road. Very big stiffy. Frozen to death."

"Why would that interest me?" I asked.

"Police think it was suicide. Maybe not. Maybe much more. Might help your reputation."

Now, to be fair to Louie, he was not often wrong in these sorts of things. I'd made a bit of a reputation the year before. A case about an illusionist. It made the back page of the newspaper and that was about it. There was no fame or fortune. No autograph signings. I mean, not all was lost. I got accepted into the Better Business Bureau, not that it made much difference. Nobody checks for that sort of shit these days. But I was asked to join the Masons. That wouldn't help much because I already knew the handshake and I don't like going to meetings.

"I'll be ten minutes," I said. "I'll check to see if any of our clients have put out a Missing Persons Report."

I thought about somebody freezing to death out there. It had been minus thirty for a couple of weeks. Was it an accident, suicide, or was it murder? I wondered why Louie had been so suspicious. Was anybody else involved? I left Rita snoring. When she woke up, she'd probably be pissed that we didn't have time for Dim Sum that day. It was part of our Saturday routine at the Imperial Palace in Calgary.

Louie arrived ten minutes later. He was suitably equipped for a day in the wilderness. Two coffees and a large box of donuts. I jumped into his Range Rover, and we set off. Now you might think that a Range Rover was ostentatious for Louie, but that was his only possession of any value. He just didn't give a shit about anything else. He liked fancy cars, and he used to like fancy women. Besides, the car held the road well and he could really speed in it. He was not too concerned about getting a ticket. After all, he could afford them, and besides, he was a cop, and cops have friends.

The Forestry Trunk Road was about 40 kilometres west of Calgary and was just the sort of place you didn't go to in the middle of winter. A few die-hards went ice fishing up there and it was an ice fisherman who had stumbled across the car. He had called the police after peering into the deserted vehicle. He had suggested that an ambulance be called, but it was a bit late for that. About two months too late.

When we pulled up to the car, the police had been there for a while doing the sorts of things they do in these situations. Most were sitting in their cars, with the heater full on. Some were huddled together, talking outside, identities partly hidden by the condensation from their breaths. It was still and relatively clear, other than the occasional fine-grained snow flurry. A car had slid off the road thirty yards ahead. It was covered in frost and snow, so it was difficult to identify the colour, but it looked to be a four-seat sedan. A few minutes later, an ambulance arrived.

We parked Louie's vehicle and topped up with some coffee before we got out to inspect the vehicle ahead. We got close enough to realize that the body in the car was not obvious, at least not as a body. It was encased in about two inches of ice. They had to break into the vehicle not because it was locked, but because it was frozen shut. It was surprising that the body had been found. The windscreen must have been opaque with frost. The driver was male and had died clutching the steering wheel.

I tried to keep out of the picture as much as I could. After all, this was temporarily a police matter, but according to the police, this was likely a suicide. They'd had a similar case the year before. That was in a much less isolated place, but nobody noticed for a couple of months. I hung around behind Louie. Nobody seemed to be too bothered.

Nothing could be done, but one of the medics asked whether they could do anything to help. I tried to be funny. I always do in these situations. Must be some sort of defence mechanism.

I said "I'd recommend 100 ccs of saline and a warm drip.........for about three months.' A voice told me to fuck off. I imagined it would take a long time before the body would thaw out completely and it would have to be gradual. Bad things would happen if you tried a quick thaw.

Once thawed out, the body might then tell a story, but one or two things gave an inkling of what could have happened. There was an empty bottle of blood thinners clutched in the deceased's hand and a typed letter on the seat by the body. It was unsigned. Not that I'm an expert, but I would assume that the drugs would be fatal. You'd probably bleed to death from numerous locations but that would have to be confirmed by the pathologist. And that was all there was. There might have been some identity in the man's pockets, but you couldn't see it because of the layer of ice covering the body. And there was a box of uneaten doughnuts on the passenger front seat. The deceased had not died with a smile on his face. I would at least have gone to my maker with a creamy donut on my lips.

The police seemed quite convinced that this was a suicide, and they seemed quite disinterested in addressing any other alternative. The next thing to do was to haul the car away and put the body into the care of the pathologist. Louie would check up on the outcome later.

I climbed back into Louie's car and finished my lukewarm coffee. I also looked at some details I had gleaned from the car. I would have to check it all out later. I thought the car was a rental or an Uber. Hopefully not the latter. If it was, where the fuck was the driver? And there was one other thing. Under the covering of ice, I could see that this guy had been wearing a face mask. He wanted to commit suicide, but obviously, he didn't want to die of COVID-19. Perhaps he thought he might not be able to get through the pearly gates if he wasn't wearing a mask. There might be no admission without a mask.

We arrived back at my house about forty minutes later. It was too late to consider Dim Sum. Rita was not a happy girl. The suggestion of a coffee at Tims, our local coffee outlet, hardly made up for it, but it allowed me to get the team together. I invited the rest of the team and that included Rita.

Let me tell you about the team. I won't include Louie. Louie was his own team. He was just about to leave the police force and was ready to start some private sleuthing. He was fiercely independent and answered to very few. A great guy but with a temper which, fortunately, was typically restrained. Our team was made up of me, Red, and Red's wife, Jen. Those two had lived in my basement for a while. Now they had married and moved into a new house in the southwest. Sometimes Rita was a part-time member of the team when she wasn't pissed off with me.

Red was the brains behind the operation. I had the pretend brains. You know the situation. You sit there trying to look intelligent, and when somebody says something smart, you nod and say what a remarkable insight that was. I was also the only one with a three-piece mohair suit. Red would always see through this crap. He once asked me for a definition of insight. I told him Insight was probably a charity for the blind. It was about the only time he peed himself laughing at one of my jokes.

Red was an imposing bloke. Red was not his real name. I think he was originally called Running Bear, but he preferred Red, so Red it was. You'd always take him seriously. Officially, he was our vice president, whatever that meant. An indigenous man of impressive stature and even more impressive erudition. That's the sort of word he'd use. Erudition. Fucked if I knew what it means. He could talk to you about anyone from Voltaire to Descartes, and you would believe him.

Red was a big bugger. He was a professional wrestler at one time. He could have been a bouncer and probably once was. The sort of guy who you'd want on your side in any argument. But he was one of the blokes. It's a guy thing. You could really slag him off and he'd either get you back with a zinger or sit there and laugh and tell you to piss off. Sorry, girls. As I said, it's a guy thing.

Jen, his wife, was a real complement to him and a veritable Jill of All Trades. Bright and athletic. She used to be a professional pole dancing instructor and still was an expert in the art. She was on a temporary assignment. It was called being pregnant and morning sickness wouldn't be helped by a plate of donuts at Tims. They lived in a rather fancy part of town. Jen had come into an unexpected inheritance that allowed them to say goodbye to our basement. They had lived there for a few months before they married. I would always tease Red. I'd tell him he had made his money the old-fashioned way. He'd married into it.

Louie was also included in the discussion. He'd just been down to the station to take soundings. He joined our conversation after a few minutes. Unofficially, of course. It was still a police investigation. He was on to his second coffee within ten minutes. It would not be long before he started on his second sausage muffin with a slice of bacon. Did I mention that Louie was a roly-poly sort of guy, though the fat hid a rather muscular frame? We used to call him the big bear, admittedly not to his face. He could rearrange your face just by looking at it.

"What do the cops think about all of this?" I said to Louie.

"Straightforwardly......open and slammed case," he replied.

"You mean suicide?"

"What else? It's the end of the month. Want to get rid of cases before Christmas."

Louie had this awkward habit of spitting his food across the table. We'd pretend not to notice.

"You have your doubts?" said Red.

"Muchly. Just call it a strange feeling in the pit of my bowels."

We knew what he meant.

"Any evidence yet?" Red said.

"Nothing except the suicide note. I photo shopper it."

Louie gave us a copy to look at. It was quite brief.

"I can't go on; this is the end. I've been a failure. All the colours out there are black."

It went downhill from there. I must admit, I'd felt like this the first time I got ditched by my girlfriend. I had a shot of whiskey then and decided that the whiskey was better than the girl. No need for me to write any notes. I finished the bottle.

I've seen too many notes like this. Anyone could write a suicide note like this one, except I just wouldn't. I'd try to make it interesting. No point in depressing the reader. You know, somebody should set up a company where you can get less depressing suicide notes downloaded from a website. Payment up front, of course.

"That's unusual," said Red. It was written using an American version of Word.

"What do you mean?" I replied.

"All the words like colour use the American spelling."

"Probably used a spell check," said Rita. "My program does that."

"A good point. But it's a bit fastidious to use spell check on your suicide note," Red said.

I didn't know the word fastidious. I just guessed the meaning. I didn't want to highlight my ignorance.

"There's another thing bothering me," I said. "Why not sign it? I mean, surely that's why you write a suicide note."

"Perhaps, he had second thoughts," said Red.

"Should have had third thinks," said Louie. "Then maybe not die. Anybody mind if I get another breakfast sandwich?" He didn't wait for a reply.

"The one thing that bothers me is why he would be wearing a mask in the car when he's on his own?" I said.

"Nothing strange about that, Sid," said Red. "Plenty of people do that. I saw this athlete running down the street the other day. I shouted that he should run faster. Said that the virus was gaining on him. He told me to fuck off. When he saw my size, he started running a lot faster."

"One other thing," said Louie, as he returned, a breakfast sandwich hidden in his paw.

"What's that?" said Rita.

"The car was an Uber. It was reported stealed about eight weeks ago."

"This must be a first," I said. "Somebody steals a car so that he can drive it into the wilderness to commit suicide."

"Perhaps he didn't have a car. Perhaps he rode a motorbike," said Rita.

"Honey, I couldn't see him riding his motorbike out there, taking the pills, and sitting on his bike to die. Perhaps, he sat there wondering if a stolen car might drive by and help him out. Still, I suppose it's a possibility, though only just." I hope she didn't realize I was taking the piss.

"So, he overdosed,' said Red. "On what? Barbiturates, painkillers, anti-depressants."

"Blood thinners, I think."

"That's right," responded Louie. "A drug that stops the blood cells gluing together. There was also a prescription bottleclutched in his hand. Empty. We'll have to wait further tests."

"So, what we have here is someone who already has a medical problem," said Red.

"Or he lived with someone who had a medical problem."

"Good point, Louie," Red replied.

"He could have been done in by a murderer with poor circulation," I said. I was joking.

"Nobody mentioned murder," said Rita.

"Bullshit," I replied. "That's what we were all thinking. Isn't it? Louie wouldn't have described it as interesting if he thought he'd done himself in."

There was silence. I took that to mean agreement. This felt a lot like murder and not suicide.

"What now?" said Rita. "Any ideas, Red?"

"Well, let's see if the police can come up with any evidence."

"When the body thaws out," I replied.

"Exactly."

"I think we should check out the guy who found him," I said. "You never know. He might have something to add to all of this."

"Lives out in Water Valley, I believe," said Louie. "Got ranch there."

"I know," I replied. "I've got his phone number. A fella called Matt Scobey."

"So, here's the plan,'" said Red. "Let's see if this might fit the profile of one of our clients who has reported a missing person. And then let's keep in touch with the police. We have to find out who this person is or was."

"Without that, we're completely fucked," I said.

"Jesus, Sidney," Rita said. "For fuck's sake, watch your language". She looked around the coffee bar. Everybody heard what she had just said.

That was my Rita. I smiled and shrugged my shoulders as if to suggest this was quite out of character. It wasn't.

"I'll give this Scobey a call," I said. "Fancy a run out in the country sweetie?"

I knew she'd say yes. I hoped my car would make it out there. There was a red light on the dashboard. It had been on for about a hundred and fifty thousand kilometres. Couldn't have been that important.... could it? Besides, Rita needed a bit of a break.

I called Scobey, and he was only too anxious to speak to me. He lived on a small spread just west of Water Valley. He organized

Sunday horse rides with breakfast for anyone interested. These days few people were.

Now I don't want you to imagine that Water Valley is a big conurbation. It is barely a hamlet. Just a few houses, a church, and the Water Valley Saloon. But popular with tourists in the summer who enjoyed getting off the beaten track. It was usually devoid of tourists in the winter, or indeed, anyone other than the few locals.

I said I would meet Scobey at the Saloon. His name rang a bell and as I pulled into the parking lot, it came to me. He had been a champion bull rider in his day. Shit, he still looked as if he could still give a bull a decent battle. I left Rita in the car with the heater full on. Believe it or not, she could be shy in these situations.

Scobey had been waiting outside the Saloon for a few minutes. Holy shit, it was still minus 30, but he didn't appear to mind. He was dressed in the type of denim that you would expect of a cowboy. So was I, for that matter. It was no time for the three-piece mohair suit. But he looked like a cowboy. I looked like a pretender. His denims followed the contours of his body. Mine were just baggy. At least I didn't put my cowboy hat on. I had a rather large head and mine never fit. It just looked weird. I only wore it at the Stampede. There were just so many others who looked weird at the Stampede.

We sat at the bar. He ordered a double whiskey on the rocks. I ordered a virgin orange juice. Doctor's orders, I'm afraid. I was following them...at least for this week.

"So, tell me," I said. "When did you first notice the car?"

I thought about calling him pardner but thought better of it. Not with an English accent. He'd see through that right away.

"Well, I first saw it about three weeks ago. I was out riding on my snowmobile when I spotted it at the side of the road. Didn't think much at first. You get the occasional snowshoer who doesn't balk at the frigid temperatures. Then two weeks ago it was still there. I really got interested a few days ago."

"Why was that?" I asked.

"Because it had been moved."

"What do you mean?"

"It looked as if somebody had tried to push it down into the lake."

"They didn't succeed," I said.

"If it had been pushed down to the lake, come the thaw, it would have dropped into forty feet of water."

"You said push. You mean by hand."

"No. It looked as if a truck had tried to push it. There were tire tracks in the snow. Course we've had a bit of snow since then, so they'll be gone by now."

"Anyway, it could have been a snowplow," I said.

"Doubt it," he replied. "Those guys are pretty responsible, and it wasn't exactly on the road."

"You checked the car?"

"I did. I didn't imagine that there would be anybody in there. But I used the exhaust from my snowmobile to melt the frost on the windshield."

"And that's when you saw the body?"

"Right. It was staring back out at me. It was pretty darn eerie. Difficult to realize it was actually a body."

"Then you called the cops."

"Right. They told me it was probably a suicide, but they would get there as soon as they could."

"If it had fallen into the lake, it still might be considered a suicide," I said.

"I suppose that's true."

"Anything else?" I replied.

"Nothing......oh, I found a card near the car. Sticking out of the snow. Jesus, I hate people leaving litter around," he said.

"You still got it?"

"I do." He reached into his breast pocket and pulled out a slightly dog-eared card.

"MMC Pharmaceuticals Research. Never heard of them," I said.

"Could be from a vet," he replied. "You get a few out here in the winter. The livestock can get stressed."

"Anything else unusual?"

"This may be irrelevant, but I found a discarded wrench in the snow just a few feet from the car. People are so careless. I think it had blood on it."

"Do you still have it?"

"I think I do. I probably threw it in my toolbox."

"I might need to see that and quickly," I said. "Seems suspicious."

"Maybe not. Probably hunters using it to kill a trapped animal," he replied. "I'd probably do that myself."

"We'd been talking for about five minutes when Rita appeared at the door."

"Need to use the loo," she said. Not the sort of word a prairie girl would use. I would, of course, use that term. My anglicisms were beginning to rub off on her.

"I hope you didn't turn off the car when you came in," I said. I sometimes had trouble starting the car in cold weather. I couldn't afford to be stranded out here. She nodded.

"Why don't you join us for a drink?" I said. "What's your poison?"

"A double gin and tonic," she replied. "Just to keep the cold out."

Once Rita joined us, we focused on social chit-chat. We even discovered that Matt was also a chuck-wagon driver. Not one of the big names, of course. That was a carrot for Rita. Her father had been a chuckwagon driver years before and though he too was not one of the big names, he was still well known. I knew it was coming. She asked for an autograph. Matt was very gracious about it, but once he'd signed the beer mat, he excused himself, noting that he had few duties on the ranch. He had horses to feed. It was a reasonable excuse. I said we'd keep in touch. Before I gave Rita the chance to order another shot, I paid the bill. As we left, I could only hope the car was still running.

It was a quiet trip home, but I could tell that something was amiss with Rita. She seemed uncomfortable. I mean, I felt uncomfortable paying the bill, but this was a different kind of uncomfortable. She'd been having problems with her leg for a few days now. She was complaining of pain and redness in her calf. There was no messing about with this sort of thing. I told her exactly what she should do. We'd have to act aggressively and consult with an expert. And we did. We contacted Dr. Google the moment we got home.

CHAPTER 2

Christmas was in two days, and it was going to be quiet this year. The social lockdown would see to that. Somebody was going to be making money out of this Covid lark. It sure wasn't going to be me and not my local barman. But you had to make the best of it. If you had a big family, you were essentially fucked. You wouldn't be seeing too many of them this year.

We decided to have a little get-together on Christmas Eve with a few friends. At the most, we only had a few friends, and that was the way we liked it. We invited Louie and, of course, Red and Jen. That was important since they were going to spend Christmas day on the reservation up north with distant relatives. It would be their last Christmas before they became a family. Rita had been charged with buying a few gifts for them. She even bought a Christmas gift for our talkative African Grey Parrot, Artie. I mean, women are so much more imaginative about buying gifts than us men. I would have no idea what to buy a parrot or Rita, for that matter.

I had known Red for years and Jen for about a year. There was rarely a cross word between us unless we played Scrabble. It became known as Squabble at our house, especially when Louie was there. He had words that were not in any dictionary, but he wouldn't take no for an answer. He could get quite emotional about the whole thing. We decided to risk it. Besides, Louie had threatened to bring a nice gift along.

We left a message for the old boy next door. He seemed to be quite deaf and lived on his own. Didn't hear a word from him and I quite forgot to get back to him. Perhaps he didn't hear a word from us if you get what I mean. I'd try to get back to him before the New Year.

Despite her pain, Rita had done us proud on Christmas Eve. She had been helped by a few glasses of sherry, but she had prepared some beautiful Christmas snacks that afternoon. It was quite a spread, but it wouldn't last long if Louie arrived early, and he did, along with a gift for the occasion. A bottle of tuica which was apparently quite popular in Romania. This stuff packed a punch. Sixty percent alcohol by volume and made from plums. You only had to sniff it and you needed a liver transplant. But Louie loved it. He walked in with his Dracula teeth and said in his broad Romanian accent, "A gift from Transylvania." We smiled. He did this every year, and we'd always laugh. We still had the bottles from the previous years. They'd never be opened. We never told him, and they weren't the things you could regift.

Once everybody had arrived, we tried to remain festive, but it was not long before we began to talk about the frozen body. It was hardly festive stuff, but Louie had a lot to tell us. The body had thawed out enough, but it left more answers than questions.

"I know you want talk about latest findings and the state of the body," said Louie. "I'll start by breaking the ice." He was not trying to be deliberately funny, but it did prompt a few chuckles. Louie didn't see the joke and looked a bit irritable for a moment.

"What can you tell us about the body?" I asked. "What did it look like?"

"You imagine a tomato being deep-frozen and suddenly thawed out. It like that. A big mess, but we got a few clues. This man was elderly and not in good health and even less good health now." This prompted even more chuckles.

"So, tell us about this ill health?"

"Big thing. It does not look like overdose. Initial tests suggest no evidence of blood thinners in blood, at least not the one we assume was in the bottle."

"Why would he have an empty bottle of blood thinners if he didn't use them?" said Jen.

"Your guess as good as mine," Louie said. "But he also had a bottle of pills in his jacket pocket. Not identified yet."

"Did the bottle of pills have a name on them? I believe that's mandatory these days."

"Did not know that. And no, the guy's name had been taken off. Very odd to me. It have pharmacy label though. CPTG am thinking."

"Anyway, could we get a copy of the label? It could tell us when the prescription was filled and to who," said Red.

"Will see what can do," Louie replied.

"So, how did he die?" I asked.

"Probably the cold," he answered. "A wind chill of minus 40 C tends to do that. But one odd thing. There was evidence of a puncture wound in his arm. No idea about that."

"Will they do an official autopsy?" Rita said.

"Have to in all these cases. Usually formality," Louie said.

"So, they're still saying suicide?"

"It looks like it, Sid."

"Any other evidence of note in the car?" said Jen.

"Well, there was plenty of gas in the car. And the car was left in neutral. Very strange."

"So, it could roll easily," I said. "Why would anyone wanting to commit suicide think of doing that? I mean, just think about it. I'm going to kill myself and, with a bit of luck, I might eventually roll into the lake."

"May not mean nothing. Perhaps it kids out there. Having fun," said Louie.

"In the middle of winter at minus 30, miles from anywhere. Most kids would be sitting in a shopping mall just hanging out. I don't think so," I said.

"Sidney. One odd thing," said Louie. "Heater was left in a full-on position. What you think Sid?"

"So, what we have here is someone who decides to commit suicide. Comes equipped with a bottle of blood thinners to help him on his way but doesn't take them. And dies by freezing despite having the heater full on. We don't even know who this character is yet."

"There were no documents in the car that identified him?" Jen said.

"No wallet?" I said.

"Nothing. A few receipts, but nothing unusual that would identify him. There was one thing they spotted on his arm. A tattoo of a tiger's head with the word 'Tiger' underneath."

"Perhaps the tattooist wasn't confident that people would be able to recognize the tiger." I laughed.

"A biker emblem?" said Jen.

"Not one I've seen," I said. "But then again, I'm no expert on biker tattoos."

"How was the deceased dressed?" said Jen.

"That was odd, my friend. He wearing frayed jeans and worn sneakers."

"Nothing odd about that, Louie," I replied.

"But man wasn't wearing a shirt. It looked like a pajama jacket. You never know these days, but it seemed weird."

"So, even with this evidence, the police still think this is a suicide?" I mused.

"Look people, this is not my case. I don't make the decisions," said an irritable Louie.

"This person has to be reported missing," said Red. "People just don't disappear like this, and nobody notices for six weeks or so. "I'm sorry officer, my husband left the house six weeks ago to buy some cigs wearing a pyjama top and I haven't seen him since. I didn't worry until now."

"Well, we do have a few cases of missing persons on our books," I said. "Could you go through them Red, and see what we've got? And I'm sure the police will do the same."

"It's worth a try," Red replied. "What if he was murdered, and the murderer was the next of kin? They would not be apt to report him missing."

"You said murderer," Jen said. "Isn't that rather jumping to conclusions?"

"It has all the markings," I said. "There are too many loose ends in all this to be anything as simple as suicide."

"Who knows," said Louie. "Heh, this is the Christmas season. Let's forget work for a couple of days and just relax. Anybody want me open the tuica? We all drink. Get happy."

There was an obvious silence until Rita saved the situation.

"Great idea, help yourself," said Rita. "We will drink a toast to Christmas, but perhaps a little later as we say goodbye to each other."

We all knew what she was getting at. Three or four glasses of that stuff and Louie would be hammered. He wouldn't be driving home tonight. With a bit of luck, he would ease into a completely relaxed state and not get too boisterous. And it went according to plan. Louie regaled us with stories of his youth. He had certainly been involved with some groups who were outside the law in Romania but claimed that was all behind him. A good thing as well, given his position with the police. He reminisced, talking about the holiday season in Romania. When he was a boy, Christmas was discouraged by the regime, but people celebrated the way we do. He talked about how they used to chase away evil spirits. I don't think he was talking about the tuica because he had never, ever, chased that away in my experience.

And then it was time for Scrabble. It was always a problem with Louie because he couldn't spell, but you just had to risk it. We split into three groups. Rita and I, who also couldn't spell, Red and Jen, who could have been world champs, and Louie, who was supposed to compete with the guy next door, who had not arrived, and who was deaf. We didn't think Louie would be at any disadvantage since we let his misspellings go. But you never knew what was coming. We were close to the end when Louie suddenly put down the word, 'pizda'. We told him it was not a proper word. I'd heard him use it before. It was a word that in English I would never use.

"It is real word," he said. "It refers to a woman's......"

"No, no!" I screamed. "We believe you, Louie."

With that, he put down the word. He got a triple score for the 'z' and won the game. That's usually how it ended with this guy. I just hoped Artie hadn't heard it. If he started repeating that, we wouldn't be inviting any Romanians around anytime soon.

That was almost the end of the night, but not quite. Because we would see nobody until after Christmas, Rita had decided to send them all off with a little gift. I had given her a clue about what everyone might be interested in. Everyone seemed satisfied, though Red was more than surprised. Remember, I had said that he was interested in philosophical writings. I told Rita that she might buy him something on the best political writings of Marx. When he opened his gift, it contained the best quotes from Groucho Marx. Not quite what he was interested in. Both Red and Jen tried hard not to laugh. They didn't quite succeed, but enough to hide it from Rita.

And that should have been the end of an enjoyable evening, except it wasn't. Just as everyone was leaving, Red turned to me and said.

"I think I might know who the frozen body is."

With that, Red and Jen turned to leave, and they were gone.

"What the fuck!!! Did you hear that, Louie?" I said.

I don't think he did. He was being helped into a taxi. He didn't look very well.

CHAPTER 3

We had a quiet time on Christmas day. That was usually the way it was. I spent much of the time considering Red's comment. Did he have a clue, or was he just taking the piss? I'd have to wait for a couple of days.

On Christmas Day, we opened up our gifts. I bought Rita a cookbook for the hurried chef, not that I thought she needed it. She never hurried when she was cooking. She bought me a set of nose, eyebrow, and ear hair clippers, probably because she thought I needed them, and I did. Artie got a perch. He could have had mine. Rita had knocked me off mine years before.

We huddled up and watched a few movies. Since the Covid affair, there was not much of a choice. We focused on comedies, not that Rita could laugh much. She was still in significant pain with her leg. It was beginning to swell alarmingly. We had tried painkillers but to no avail. It would need a visit to the doctor to sort things out. Of course, she would be deemed non-essential and probably not worthy of immediate help. And sitting in the hospital emergency department for four hours was not going to help. Besides, the weather was bloody awful. There was a blizzard and hurricane-like winds. We might not even get there, and we certainly wouldn't get back.

I did have a surprise though on Boxing Day night. We had just started a movie and true to form, I had fallen asleep when the doorbell went. It was Red and Jen. The weather had caused a serious power outage on the reservation, and they wondered if they could stay overnight. Hell, that wouldn't be a problem. As I said, they used to live in our basement, and it was still there, just as they had left it months before. Rita took Jen into the kitchen and it gave me a chance to ask Red about his comment a few days previously.

"So, you think you know who the frozen man is?" I said.

"I think I said I might know. Course we'd have to check it out."

"Don't leave me hanging. Check what out?"

"A couple of weeks ago, remember that woman who came to see us?" he replied. "She was looking for her father."

"Don't recall it."

"She was a theatre impresario across Canada."

"What the fuck is an impresario?" I enquired.

"Finances big stage shows."

"No, I still don't remember her," I said.

"She was worth millions."

"Holy shit. Now, I remember. She certainly had money that woman. What was her story again?"

"When her parents divorced, her mother got a big settlement. Her father got fuck all. He eventually disappeared from sight and apparently, he met hard times. They completely lost touch, which was a real pity, at least for him."

"Why was that?"

"He came into an inheritance. There's a few hundred thousand waiting for him in a lawyer's account. It's making a few grand every year in interest."

"Why do you think he's our boy?"

"The tattoo on the leg. The tiger's head. That was the only distinguishing mark."

"An odd tattoo," I said. 'How does this relate to this guy?"

"I was told that the old man played lead guitar for an early heavy metal band called Tiger."

"These days he'd be covered from head to toe in weird tattoos," I said.

"Anyway, she had paid us a retainer to find this guy with a nice bonus for finding him. I know it's a long shot."

"How much was the retainer?"

"Five grand," replied Red.

"Fuck. I didn't know about the retainer. Rita looks after the finances. So, where do we find this woman?" I said.

"She lives out in Bragg Creek. Apparently, a big mansion. We should visit her out there. If she came to

   our office, she would probably insist on being debugged, dewormed, and sanitized."

"O.K I realize that our suite of offices............."

"A suite of offices? Bullshit! An office and a toilet that doesn't flush," Red interrupted. We both laughed.

That was why I interviewed her out in Bragg Creek a few weeks ago."

"Why don't we e-mail her and say that our extensive team of operatives have come up with an important lead?"

"And we should suggest a meeting tomorrow."

"Right. And we turn up in a rented Merc. No way I can turn up in my old banger. I'll let you get on that,

   Red."

"Let's check what's available out there." He went over to my computer to open up the internet.

"What's the password, Sid?" he said.

"Password."

"Yes, what's the password?"

"Password."

"Holy shit, man. You don't use the word 'password', do you?"

"Red, do you think I'm stupid? The 'P' is in capitals." Red started laughing.

"I sometimes wonder about you, Sid. Anyway, you've got some messages in your inbox. Want me to open it up?"

"Sure, why not?"

"Holy shit, Sidney, what the hell is 'Hot Chicks.com?' Interesting site."

"Red, I know what you're thinking, but you're wrong. I was thinking of buying a new parrot for Rita. She's thinking of breeding Artie." Now I reckon you and everyone else wouldn't buy this, but it was true.

"All right, I believe you," Red said. "Seven billion people in the world wouldn't."

"Seven billion people with dirty minds," I replied. "Seven billion and one, if I include you."

"Look, there's an e-mail here from Louie. Want me to look?"

"Yeah, why not? That guy was probably in the office on Christmas day. Bloody workaholic. What's he up to?" I said.

"Apologized for using a naughty word at Scrabble, though he can't remember what it was."

"Wow, that's a first. Louie apologizing. I'm not going to tell him what it was. Anything else?"

"Yeah, the autopsy results came in. Apparently......holy crap......"

"What's that?" I said.

"The frozen man died of natural causes before he froze to death."

"How the fuck did they work that out?" I said.

"Dunno. There's a lot of medical stuff here. But it seems as if he was suffering from serious blood clots in the lungs, which eventually killed him. Is that natural?"

"This is getting even more bizarre," I said. "I mean, just think about it. A man who is already half dead drives out into the wilderness, where he commits suicide by freezing to death and tries to make people think he took an overdose. Any ideas Red?"

"Don't look for an explanation from me, but it could still be murder. There's usually money involved in all these cases. I mean, I don't see it in this case. But it will be there somewhere. You can bet on it."

"If the police think the guy died of natural causes, they sure as hell will close the file. Probably already have," I replied.

"Why would they bother to keep the case open?" said Red. "It would be a real stress on their overstretched resources, especially when they are getting all these Covid demonstrations."

"Talking about money, we should make sure that we contact...... what was her name?"

"Elizabeth Connors."

"And make sure she hears from us and not the police. Make her think we're right on the case. I don't mean to be crass, but this could be a decent payday for us."

"Heh Sid, crass is your second name. I'll get right on it. Let's say we meet her mid-morning, so we don't have to pay for lunch."

"Now that's crass," I said.

We were all early to bed that night, and hopefully, everyone slept soundly. Rita did not. She tossed and turned and was obviously in some pain. I made sure she had a decent supply of painkillers and hot pads. None of it did much good. By the time morning came, I decided it was time to contact her doctor. There was no answer. He would be away for a few days. If she thought she had Covid, she should go immediately to the hospital. If it was something else, she should call the Health Line. I would attend our meeting, but if she was not better by the afternoon, it would have to be the hospital. At least, she would travel in style. We had rented the Merc for a day.

The next morning we picked up the car, but it came with one problem. It was a stick shift, and I hadn't driven one in years. It was a matter of economy. Stick shifts were cheaper. Red had never driven one. I did my best in driving the thirty kilometres to Bragg Creek simply by not changing gears very much. Essentially, I drove all the way there in third gear, but we got there eventually. We stopped in Bragg Creek for a coffee. Lovely little hamlet Bragg Creek. Situated on the banks of the Elbow River, it was the sort of place that people would drive their cars out to on a Sunday morning and a few had this morning. The river had begun to freeze over.

The Covid pandemic had hit the few businesses there quite hard, but a few had survived. Thank god, the coffee house was still open. A steaming mug of coffee charged our spirits, and we set off. The Connors' house was about ten minutes away and was situated down a long driveway shaded by trees. Although a bit dated in style, it must have been worth a few million.

Mrs. Connors answered the door herself via an intercom. This place was well protected. There was a fairly obvious security camera over the door. I half expected a butler. Connors was in late middle age, but then again, most senior ladies describe themselves as being in late middle age. Hell, I was in late middle age, for that matter. She was very well put together though, and emanated the sort of class I could only dream of. Didn't see any sign of plastic surgery, but I'm hardly an expert on that sort of thing.

She eyed Red. I'd say lasciviously, but perhaps she just squinted a bit. She scarcely looked at me at all. Probably a bit overwhelmed by my three-piece mohair suit. Before you get the idea that I bought this thing new, I'll be honest. I bought it for five bucks at a thrift store. You might mock, but I knew an Oil Exec who bought all his suits this way and always looked smart.

Mrs. Connors invited us into her lounge, or maybe one of them. Impressive furniture. Not the sort you have to screw together yourself. We refused her offer of tea, but I munched on the biscuits. We got down to brass tacks right away. It seemed that she had not seen her father in twenty-five years. Apart from simply wanting to get in touch with him again, she told us that there was an inheritance of half a million coming his way if only we could find him. Red jumped in and asked where the money would go if her father was not found. She admitted that it would go to her.

We asked why she thought he might be in Calgary. She remembered there had been a phone call from Calgary a few years back, but she didn't have the phone number and didn't even know whether he was still alive. If he was, he would be about seventy years old.

She wondered why we might have found him. There was no way to be delicate about this. We told her about the tiger tattoo. She was quite upset with our news, but we told her we still had to identify the body. We wondered if she could come and view the body right away, and she agreed. It was a half-hour drive to the police pathologist back in Calgary, and we made it, albeit, largely in third gear. Since we did not have a name, we described the circumstances of the death to the pathologist's assistant and she was able to direct us to the location. I had no intention of scouting around through multiple bodies to find the right one. When I thought about it, the whole thing was ironic. The poor guy had died, then was frozen, then thawed out and then put back in the freezer. Holy shit, he might end his days in an incinerator.

The body was identified by a number. When they slid 9365 out on the table, it had an immediate impact. I thought I was going to throw up, but Mrs. Connors was made of sterner stuff. The corpse was not in a good state, but she was able to identify him right away. No tears, no apparent sadness. I think she had prepared herself for this. At least he had a name now. We hoped it would be Connors. If I was to be buried, I would want it to be with my name attached.

We attempted to sympathize with Mrs. Connors. But what can you say? We offered to buy her a cup of tea and a donut at Tims, but she declined. It was at times like this that I wished I had brought one of the girls along. The girls are so much better at this sort of thing. The fact that I couldn't drive a stick shift didn't help. On the way back to Bragg Creek, after struggling with getting it into gear for about a minute, she offered to drive. I said that the gearbox was a load of crap, but she didn't have any problem with it and drove us back to her mansion. When we arrived back there, we didn't go in, but there was one question we had forgotten to ask. Just what was the deceased's name? I assume it was Connors. She said Connors was her married name, though she was now divorced. Our victim's name was Sykes.

Kevin Sykes. While it seemed that the police assumed he had died of natural causes, we weren't that convinced. After she cut us another cheque, albeit smaller than the first, we were motivated to continue the investigation and she agreed to finance our efforts for the next ten days. We said that we would find out what his circumstances were and how this had all happened. If there was anything to find out, our extensive network of operatives would sort it out. She looked at us sceptically but so long as she was cutting cheques that didn't bounce, we wouldn't be too sensitive.

As we drove back, the gearbox suddenly became difficult again. I couldn't wait to get into my old Chevy and once we picked it up, we decided we would meet up at Red's house. It was time to get everyone together especially Louie, if he was available. We called him from the car, and he said he did have a few moments to spare. Red and Jen lived just behind Calgary Olympic Park. You could see the outline of the ski jump from their front door. Their house looked as if it had come straight out of Modern Living.

You might have worked this out, but unlike Red and Jen, I had little time for modern décor. I was never going to pay over five hundred dollars for a sofa. If it was bright pink, so be it. Our garage was filled with junk and on a good day, it would be impossible to get the door shut. I mean, that was it. No pretensions in our house. Red and Jen were made of different stuff. No srew it together shit. When they got married, I gave them a gift certificate for five hundred dollars for one of those places. I am not sure they ever used it. Heh, it's the thought that counts.

When we got there, Jen had this fancy flavoured coffee just percolated, waiting for us. It was fine if you liked that sort of stuff. I preferred Tims, to be honest. And I liked it out of a cardboard cup. I called Louie to see how long he would be. He was on his way, but he was able to tell me about something that might break the case wide open. There had been a set of fingerprints found on the steering wheel of the car. The police assumed they were the victims. Louie had a feeling they weren't. He had decided to see if he could get a match. I also asked him to find out if anyone had taken life insurance out on the deceased man. It would take a few days to find out about that.

We sat around sipping coffee. Let's face it. You don't drink that stuff; you sip it. I passed on the biscuits. I think they call them biscotti. Not good when you're wearing a plate.

It was clear that the events of the day had moved the case forward. We now knew who the deceased man was. If he was murdered, we would have to find a motive. That was always the first step. The issue was who would want to hide his death and why. We decided we would do a full-court press to find out more about Kevin Sykes. All our operatives, which meant Red and I with an assist from Jen and encouragement from Rita, would get going. Our first task was to discover where Sykes had lived and whether he had any other next of kin. That would have to wait until the morning, and it might be difficult. There were probably quite a few Kevin Sykes in Calgary and more than quite a few in Alberta. But things would have to wait for now. Rita had called me and told me she was really feeling unwell. I gave my apologies and headed home.

When I got home, Rita was stretched out on the sofa. She was running a temperature and had a lot of pain. Rita was never one to complain. She was one of those breed of women out there who would say, "Fuck it, I'll take an aspirin and be fine by the morning." I said, "Fuck it, we're going to the hospital right now." So off we went. The hospital car park was empty when we got there. Even the section devoted to Covid patients was empty. Odd. I thought we had a pandemic. The Emergency Department seemed as if it was half-staffed. It possibly didn't need any more staff. There was hardly anyone there. And we got seen quickly. Two and a half hours didn't seem long to wait. I once waited for six hours to see a doctor. It was just before my heart attack. He said I was suffering from anxiety and to go away and take something to relax. So, I did. I picked up a bottle of Johnie Walker and took a few shots. He was right. It made me feel better despite the chest pain.

Rita was taken into an examination room and examined by a young doctor. They seem to get younger by the year, or perhaps it's just me getting older. She was away for about an hour. I mean, after half an hour you get to worry. Clearly, we weren't talking about hemorrhoids, jock itch, halitosis, or premature baldness. This could be serious.

After about an hour, they emerged. Rita did not look at all impressed. The doctor informed us she had something called phlebitis. Not serious, but it could be. I didn't know much about medical matters. To me, it sounded as if she had inflammation of the phlebes, wherever they were. She would have to take medication, and that was it.

It was a case of seeing your doctor if he's available, but remember, you're non-essential. And remember no vigorous physical activity. So, it would hardly impact our sex lives one way or the other. There was one further option. It was rumoured that a new research clinic in town had come up with a new exciting treatment. I mean, I would have been comfortable with a boring old treatment that worked, but this one paid you to be involved. Rita seemed interested and by the time we got home, she decided to take up the offer. The organization was called Micro Medical Corporation, and it seemed that they could get you in right away. I opened up the computer when we got home and checked the prescription we'd been given. I discovered that this stuff was the same as the stuff used in rat poison.

"I think I'll pass on that shit," she said.

"Not a bad idea. Sometimes, the cure is worse than the illness. Do you know how many people are killed by prescription meds every year?" I replied.

I don't and I'm not sure I want to know," she muttered.

"Anyway, you up for this MMC company, love?" I said.

"Why not?" she replied. "It'll buy me some new curtains for the kitchen. I'll call the clinic up first thing in the morning."

"So, what are you going to do tonight?" I said.

"Fuck it, I'll take an aspirin and be fine by the morning".

"Honey, I think we need to do more just to be safe," I said.

"Fuck off ..... fuck off!"

I turned to look at Rita and we both turned to look at the parrot. I can't imagine where Artie got those words from. That's what happens when you adopt one of those birds. You don't know where they've come from, and from now on, we'd have to be careful of any potty mouths coming through the door.

CHAPTER 4

Bowness was not always part of Calgary. It was its own separate enclave cut off from Calgary by the Bow River. Nowadays, it is considered to be almost an inner part of the city. Still, it's an interesting place, Bowness. A strange mix of rich and poor. To the north are the fancy houses by the river. The rest is dominated by low-cost housing or as I like to call it economic housing.

The area is separated by a high street which saw a bit of a revival at the turn of the century. Many small shops emerged on the high street and though it never became a shopper's paradise, you could find some nice eateries and pubs along the main drag, despite Covid. It also had one other less desirable aspect. For a time, it was home to the Hell's Angels. Their headquarters looked like a fort. It really did. I believe they were persuaded to move by the police, though I have no idea where. I should add. I wouldn't have been the one to persuade them.

This was where Kevin Sykes used to live. It wasn't any great detective work to find out where. He was actually in the electronic phonebook. All the other Kevin Sykes were no longer in the city, and when they were, they were too young. We tried calling his number a few times, but there was no answer. Reasonable, I suppose, because he was dead, but we got to hear his voice through messaging. Even so, we decided to drive down to where he last lived. He might have been living with someone who might add some fresh insights into his demise.

Kevin lived in what I would have described as a 1960s bungalow. Needed a lick of paint, but the garden looked well organized. It had gone into a deep freeze a couple of months back, but there would be a maze of perennials pushing through in a few months. There was also a mini-library just off to the side of the garden. This was a box-like structure where people would place used books for others to read.

When we knocked at the door, it was opened by an unpretentious middle-aged woman, except for the dyed blonde hair and the cigarette in her fingers. A definite '60s feel about this lady. Still, you wouldn't have noticed her in Walmart. We asked if we could talk to her about Kevin. She nodded as if to say she knew him. She invited us in. The lounge area was decorated in a way that would not have looked out of place in my house. Sure, it was cheap, but it was neat and tidy. Had a bit of a musty smell that often comes with age. Might have been the two cats that were sitting beside her on the sofa. I briefly introduced myself.

"It's very nice to meet you.... er...Mrs.?"

"Bowyer. Lila Bowyer. And you are?'

"Sidney Arbuckle, Lou Diamond Investigations, and my lead in-vestigator." I glanced at Red.

"I know Kevin's dead," she said. "The police called me earlier this morning." That was interesting. I wondered how they got the jump on us."It must have been a shock," I said.

"Not really. I wasn't surprised. Where was he going to go?"

"What was your relationship with Kevin?" said Red.

"Not exactly common law, but not exactly strangers. I met him about six years ago. He was a bit down on his luck at the time. He'd been in the Hells Angels for a few years but had given that up. I met him outside one day. He used to borrow books from the box outside, and that was several times a week. He was obviously an avid reader. I felt quite sorry for him, so I offered him my spare room in the basement. We found we had quite a bit in common and he was very useful around the house."

"Did he pay rent?" I said.

"For a while he did, but after some time I was just glad to have him here. He had his uses," she said. Sounded like most of the marriages I knew, at least the ones that lasted.

"When did you first become aware of his absence?" I said.

"About five or six weeks ago."

"And you didn't report him missing?"

"Look, I know it seems unusual, but Kev often went away. He occasionally did some long-distance driving. Sometimes he'd be away for a couple of months. Sometimes he'd call me. Sometimes he wouldn't."

"Did he ever show any signs of being depressed?" Red enquired.

"Well, everyone gets down from time to time. He sometimes would drink too much but he certainly wasn't suicidal if that's what you're asking."

"We never mentioned suicide," I said.

"The police did," she replied. "And they were quite persistent about it."

"So, there were no signs that he might want to harm himself?'

"He hadn't been very well, but I put that down to age. I know that he had sought medical help in the past. I think he saw a psychiatrist a few years back. These days, if you're non-essential, it's difficult to get the help you need, and he certainly couldn't afford to pay for a psychologist. But I couldn't imagine that he would ever kill himself." I'd heard that story so many times before from the next of kin. Suicide could be quite unexpected.

"Did he have a will?" said Red. I knew Red would go in that direction.

"I'm not sure he had much to leave. He earned just enough to survive. Never talked about a will. Why would he? I suppose there was his record collection," she said.

"Record collection," said Red. He had probably never seen a vinyl record before.

"Yes, he had this turntable and a collection of classical records. Might be worth something to a collector, I suppose. I'm more country and western, so I made him play them downstairs."

It was unlikely in my view that the guy would make a will just for a few records. Red knew his classical music. Might be a buyer there.

"Do you know anybody who might want to harm him?"

"He was involved with the Hells Angels at one time, but I doubt that was an issue any longer. So, to answer your question, I'd say no. He didn't really have any friends. Just a few acquaintances. And he never had visitors. But he was a gentle soul. I can't imagine anyone having any malice towards him, though."

"Well, thank you for answering our questions," said Red. "If you can think of anything else, that might help us give me a call." He handed her one of our cards.

"I certainly will, Mr. Diamond," she said. I realized I hadn't introduced Red to her. He smiled.

As we drove home, we both concluded that Mrs. Bowyer probably had nothing to hide. She was not involved in a loving relationship. Probably one of convenience. Perhaps most were these days.

When we got home, there was a message waiting for us from Louie. He told Rita that the police had come up with a possible match for the fingerprints that had been found on the steering wheel of the car. He didn't say whose they were. We'd have to wait a little while to find out. If they were not Kevin's, we might be on to something.

Rita had called the MMC clinic earlier that morning, and they had agreed to interview her right away. Her initial interview meeting was down at their clinic in Market Mall, and we only had a few minutes to get there. Boy, these guys were in a hurry. If we had gone through a specialist we probably would have had to wait six months.

I had lived in Calgary for 40 years, so I knew how to avoid most of the traffic lights on the way to the clinic in the northwest quadrant of the city. I knew where to slow down at the photo-radar hotspots simply because I used to monitor these roads when I was a cop. We got there with a couple of minutes to spare.

The MMC clinic was just what you might expect. Expensive décor, an expensive receptionist, and expensive furniture that would have looked quite at home at Red and Jen's. I expected we wouldn't have to wait long. Public satisfaction at these places is always paramount, at least in the early stages until the guaranteed contracts come in. They were obviously interested in us taking part in their trial, and quickly. I was right. There was money to be made here. Most of it by them, I assumed, but there was some left over for participants.

Within moments, a rather supercilious and well-coiffured gent in a white coat greeted us. He had a stethoscope around his neck, so it seemed as if he was a doctor. Except he wasn't. He introduced himself as Lance, the assistant researcher on the project. His card indicated an affiliation with the university. He had what I described as a posh English accent. That always made me uncomfortable. My accent was rather unposh.

Lance took us into the inner sanctum of the clinic, where we were introduced to Dr. Lawrence Berryman. His office was what you might expect. Plush carpet, a mahogany desk, a couple of sculptures, and several abstract paintings that looked like they had been painted by an elephant. Perhaps they had. I thought that he came across as a bit of a used car salesman but to be fair; he was trying to sell us on the merits of his new drug. But Rita was impressed. Did I say he was good-looking and was wearing expensive shoes? His haircut probably cost more than my car, which was probably not saying that much.

"Well, it's very nice meeting you, Rita. And?" He looked at me quizzically.

She was quite capable of saying my chauffeur or something, but she resisted the temptation. She knew I would have pissed myself laughing.

"This is my intended," she said with a smile. That was almost worse.

"Intended for what?" he said and let out a snigger. This guy wasn't scoring any points with me.

"My husband," she said indignantly. "It's Sidney."

"Well, we always like to have the next of kin attend these appointments. It shows support and empathy. Caring always leads to a good outcome in these cases."

This guy was velvety smooth. He could probably sell a packet of condoms to the Pope.

"How much will we be paid for this?" I said. I wanted to get down to the really important stuff early.

"If you, or rather your intended, finish the trial, you could expect up to five hundred dollars." That could buy a nice sofa, I thought, but I knew Rita wanted curtains.

"We'll sign on the dotted line," said Rita. I wasn't convinced about this before we had seen a contract, but it was her body, after all.

"We will, of course, have to run some tests and take a full medical history. We will have to do that privately, but it's nothing more than a formality. Which means that your...."

"I'll have to bugger off," I said. He nodded. He didn't seem to be particularly amused by my bluntness. I can't imagine why.

"You might want to look at some of our brochures." He was looking at me. It will answer all your questions." He thrust a few pamphlets at me. He didn't give me much of an option to refuse. It's in quite simple language that you'll be able to understand," he said. This guy was a complete dick. I'd read them once I got home.

I left the office and sat outside in the reception area. I worried about Rita signing a contract that she would probably skim through at best. There were several magazines on the coffee table, but Continental Holidays, Modern Décor and Furniture, European Hairstyles, and French Fashions were not on my agenda. I went outside the office to pick up another magazine. I chose the Calgary Sun. That too was in clear and simple language, but it also had pictures.

Rita and Dr. Berryman appeared in the reception area about an hour later. There was just time for me to finish the crossword. He did all the talking.

"Well, we've run some preliminary tests, and it looks as if Rita meets all the requirements for the study." Now there was a shock. "It will mean a couple of days in a private ward just to assess progress," he said. "And then she'll feel fine."

"What if she doesn't?" I enquired.

"We're very confident about our new product, Xyloleptokinase," he said.

"I beg your pardon," I replied.

"I'm sorry. That's the chemical name. It's based on an extract of radish root. We prefer to call it Radishon Co-factor. It was all in the information I gave to you. I'm sure you read it." I was sure I hadn't

"Very interesting," I replied. "Can't you just eat a lot of radishes?"

"You could, but you would have to eat a few tons in one sitting and that would certainly kill you."

"Who discovered it?" I said.

"It was one of our French research scientists. Radishon has become very popular in France. Illegal, I must admit, since it has not been licensed there yet."

"So, it's not a made-up chemical," I said. "It's completely natural?"

"Absolutely. And we've had some great testimonies from some quite famous people. Patti Laviolette, the famous film star, for example. She was on her back until she started using Radishon Co-Factor."

I bet she was, I thought. Most of those young film stars spent a good deal of their time on their backs looking for their next part. I said nothing. I decided that discretion was the better part of valour.

"How do you take this stuff?" I said. It was a good question. "Is it a pill, or an injection, or do they insert them in the French way?

"The French way?"

"Doesn't matter," I replied. This guy looked as if he might be offended, at least the way I would have described it.

"A couple of injections and then pills for a week. Thereafter, you only need to take one pill every week if you need it.'

"You didn't answer my first question," I said.

"Which was?"

"What happens if it doesn't work?"

"Well, we can rely on the older, more expensive medications." A new medication that is cheaper, I thought to myself. I wasn't buying that, but I kept quiet.

"When do I have to come in?" said Rita. She seemed enthusiastic. I know she was thinking of the money and we needed the new curtains right away.

"Well, if you come down to the clinic tomorrow afternoon, we can process you and you'll be out in a couple of days. I have to tell you, it will feel like a holiday abroad. We have international chefs to look after your nutritional needs and a beautician to look after your female requirements."

I wasn't sure what female requirements were. Probably leg waxing, teeth whitening, Botox injections, and foot massages. There might be lectures on how to snag a millionaire. But Rita deserved it. She worked her arse off. If it helped, I was all for it.

"We'll be there at....what time?" said Rita.

"Let's say 2.30," said Berryman. "I'll let my receptionist show you people the door."

I mean, we could see where the door was. He was just telling us to fuck off. She stepped forward to usher us out. It was quite obvious to me that the receptionist, for one, wasn't complexly natural. Rita saw me looking at the unnatural bits and gave me a quick dig in the ribs. She pushed me out of the door.

I know we had decided to take part, but I thought we should talk it over. What better place than Tims? There was one just across the road. I bought the coffee while Rita read the literature we'd been given. There was a long lineup. She'd have read the brochures before I got back.

When I returned with the coffee, Rita was beaming. I knew she was still ill and in some pain, but her face showed some hope. She seemed impressed.

"I think this is a real opportunity," she said. "It was such a lovely office"

"But can they actually help you?" I replied.

"I think so," she said. "The clinical trials have been positive."

Now you might think I am too negative, but who said they were positive? Some dude given a grant to say just that. I let it pass.

"There's obviously a lot of money behind this venture." Rita continued. "Apparently, a lot of people have been investing in the company. There's a form here that allows you to buy shares in the company at a discount. Course, we'd need a broker." I had one but hadn't talked to him in years.

"I suppose we could think about that," I said. "Mrs. Connors is still paying us a nice fee and we do have money in the bank."

"Dr. Berryman told me he was hoping to go on Nasdaq."

"What's that," I said. "Is that a natural substance extracted from five tons of bullshit?"

She looked at me and laughed and then told me to fuck off. That parrot was proving to be a terrible influence on the girl.

CHAPTER 5

I definitely didn't mean to focus on the case when we got home. Rita's comfort was primary in my mind, but Red had called me and said he was coming over. This was partly because he had some new information but also because he had a strong affinity for Rita. In the early days, Rita had been a bit of a mother substitute for Red and he'd never forgotten it.

When I got home, Red was sitting in our lounge. He had a key to the house, so he'd let himself in. He gave Rita a big hug. I suggested she go and lie down. She wanted to make Red a sandwich. He said that he had just eaten a sandwich, though I knew he hadn't. We insisted she lie down and when she did, we discussed the news that had just come in.

"What have you got for me, Red?"

"Apparently, Mrs. Connors had taken out a life insurance policy on her father a little while back," he said. God knows how he had found this out so quickly, but I told you he was smart.

"You're shitting me. How much was it for?" I asked.

"Two hundred and fifty thousand dollars."

"Jesus. That's a lot of moolah," I said.

"Sid, to me and you it would," said Red. "To her, maybe not. Chump change. Might be the year's interest in her investments."

"Do they know when it was taken out?" I replied.

"I think it was about five weeks ago."

"Just a minute. It seems as if our boy may actually have died before that. No cigar on that one.'"

"That's right," said Red. "A bit like betting on a horse race after it's finished."

"And a dead racehorse at that," I said.

"Nice analogy, pardner," Red suggested.

"But why would she do that?" I replied. "I mean, it's pretty obvious that she must have suspected that he might be dead. And for somebody, she says she hadn't seen for years. This doesn't make any sense at all. To say the least, the timing is a bit more than suspicious. There's no such thing as coincidence when crime is involved, at least in my view."

"Just a lucky guess, I suppose. If she didn't know where he was and where he died, how could she possibly put in a claim?" Red replied. "Unless she was lying through her expensive teeth."

"But why bring suspicions on herself by reporting him missing?"

"What do you think we should do about this, Sid? I mean, at the very least, she has to know that we found out about the life insurance."

"I'm sure she could come up with an excuse, though god knows what it could possibly be," I said

Red then attempted to imitate Mrs. Connors. He had a real ear for this sort of thing.

"Not a problem gentleman, I had this dream that my father was going to die, so I took advantage of the situation and took out life insurance. I was going to give the money to a deserving charity. No need to be paranoid, gentlemen, is there?"

"Look Red, if he was already dead, the policy would be void," I said.

"That's a good point," he replied. "Why don't we check out this woman's background on the computer? Let's fire it up and see what we can get."

My laptop was sitting on the kitchen table. It had been left on all day. In fact, it may have been on for much longer. Most days we simply couldn't be bothered turning it off and I'm told that is not necessarily a bad thing. Once we had gotten out of Rita's last website entitled 'Terrible culinary disasters you want to avoid,' we decided to find out more about Mrs. Connors.

Would we find her on Wikipedia? We could. Of course, you always ran the risk with Wikipedia that what you were reading was not completely true. The picture of Mrs. Connors was not completely accurate. I am no expert on photoshopping, but she looked as if she had lost fifteen years since we saw her. My bet was on this. Perhaps it was Calgary's very dry climate. Perhaps it wasn't. Perhaps it was expensive makeup. Who knows?

We found out quite a lot about this lady. She had been involved in many excursions into the field of business. She had started as an impresario probably on the back of her mother's money. She had financed quite a few successful musical shows in Toronto and one on Broadway. She had become a bit of a TV personality for a while and was a regular on talk shows. She hosted a show about entrepreneurs called ' Get your business plan right or you're screwed.' And she'd appeared several times on some of the popular cooking shows. Rita would probably have seen her on the TV.

She obviously hadn't worked on her business plan for ' Get your business plan right or you're screwed.' because the show only lasted six episodes. Thereafter, she sat on numerous boards. They were in many fields including technology, mining, medical research, publishing, and film production. There was a whole list of them. She had even been elected to the board of a hedge fund. In bold letters, it told us of all the charitable organizations she had donated to. All very nice in my view but at the end of the day, it was still a tax write-off. There wasn't much of a personal nature on the site except that her first husband had been tragically killed in a boating accident. We'd assume for the time being that it was an accident.

"Order of Canada next, I expect and a probable seat in the Senate," Red said. "Probably in the next seat to you, Sid." He chuckled.

"Well, I'll tell you one thing," I replied. "Her next TV program might be called 'Get your alibi right' or you're completely fucked' or words to that effect."

"I'm not sure I want to drive out to Bragg Creek today," Red said. "The chinook has made the roads very treacherous. Some of the roads are flooded in parts. Where they're not, they're ankle-deep in slush. I think we should call her and put her on speaker."

"I agree," I said. "Let me dial. I'll use my personal phone. I think it's time to be blunt with this lady."

I took her card out of my wallet. It was quite modest, really. I expected it to be gold embossed with a list of her academic qualifications. There were none listed. Then again, many financially successful people don't incur the cost of university education. Why be burdened for the rest of your life with debt? In my view, I have to ask whether many university courses are worth it. My old man seemed to have worked it out. He used to say, "Life is not a multiple-choice test, son." Very insightful, if you ask me. That philosophy never harmed me, at least when my memory was working.

I didn't think Connors would be there, but she answered it on the second ring.

"Hello, Mr. Arbuckle. What can I do for you?'" she said. She obviously had a call display, and she did get the name right.

"We're continuing our investigation into your father, and we are making some progress."

"I'm so glad to hear it. Did you find out how my father died? I mean, before he froze to death."

"We have some leads, but that's not exactly why we're calling Mrs. Connors. I have my colleague Red here."

"Good morning Mrs. Connors," Red said.

"Hello, Mr. Diamond," she replied. "Nice to talk to you again." No point in correcting her.

"During our investigation we discovered, or we think we discovered, that you took life insurance on your father," said Red. "Is that true?"

"Yes, it is, Mr. Diamond. That's very good sleuthing. I'm impressed. But there is a perfectly good explanation for this."

"I'm glad to hear it," said Red. "And the explanation is?" I needed to hear this.

"I have done this sort of thing before. I usually give the money to charity, and it defrays any funeral expenses. "

"Usually or always," I said

"Always. The last time I did this was for my brother. I think you'll find it all checks out. I can give you the name of the charity if you like. It'll pay off any of his debts and funeral expenses."

"But why now?"

"Coincidence, I suppose," she replied. There was that word again.

"Funerals don't usually cost two hundred and fifty thousand dollars, Mrs. Connors," said Red. "That's a very expensive coffin."

"It won't cost anything like that now," she replied.

"Why is that?" said Red.

"He is to be cremated in a couple of days. I doubt there will be many people attending. It won't be an open coffin. I think you quite understand why."

"Indeed, I do," I replied.

"And I should add that the insurance policy was void because the insurance company indicated that my father had died before I took the insurance out."

"I see," said Red.

"Have you people any further information on my father's last days?"

"Not yet, Mrs. Connors, but we are making good progress," I said. I'm not sure what progress I was referring to. She'd have to believe we were. We hadn't deposited her last cheque. It might be a good idea if we did so quickly. I had a bad feeling about all of this.

"We will get back to you if we hear anything, Mrs. Connors," I said.

"Thank you, gentlemen. This has been painful for me," she said. Missing out on two hundred and fifty grand would certainly have been painful for me.

"Take care," I replied. I looked at Red. He nodded, and I ended the call.

"What do you think, young fella?" I said.

"Complete bollocks if you ask me. I mean, who the heck gave her the idea that her father was dead or about to die? Work that out and we may have solved the mystery."

"You're too cynical. I mean, it could be true."

"Could be."

"The issue is, what do we do now?" I replied.

"Absolutely nothing, boss."

"Nothing. Why the fuck not?"

"Because we have a shitload of other stuff to do. What I'd suggest is taking our surveillance vehicle down to Bragg Creek in the morning. We can find out who Mrs. Connors is associating with. Maybe nobody of importance, but it would be nice to find out."

I thought Red was being paranoid but then again; you had to be in this business. Nothing ventured, nothing gained, as my father used to say. Connors didn't look like a murderer to me, but in family affairs, none of them ever did.

"Could you do the surveillance?" I said. "I'll be taken up with making sure that Rita gets to the clinic on time. She'll be pissed if I'm not around."

"Afraid not. I've got a meeting with Louie. Some fast-breaking news, or so he informs me."

"Not that fast-breaking if it has to wait until tomorrow."

"Look, old fella. I'll ask Jen if she would consider going out to Bragg Creek tomorrow morning."

"But she's a bit pregnant," I said.

"Sidney, my friend. You can't be a bit pregnant. You're either pregnant or not. I can assure you she is."

"Is it wise, though?"

"Don't see why not," he replied. "She's only twelve weeks along. A friend of hers ran a marathon at thirty-four weeks. I've talked to her about this sort of thing. Look, she's bored shitless. She wants to get involved again. No harm in asking."

"Alright, if she agrees. We'll send her to Bragg Creek in the surveillance vehicle," I said.

Now I'd have to admit we'd had some unlikely surveillance vehicles in our time. We had started with a van that had Walid's Falafels on the side. That sort of stood out too much. Besides, people kept asking if we had any falafels. Then we got an old school bus with no seats. That sort of worked, but we kept getting waved down by parents who wanted to get their children on the bus. Our latest edition was a truck that looked like one of those lawn maintenance trucks. I mean you would see them everywhere in the summer but not in the winter. We'd forgotten about that. I mean, we could have said we were doing snow removal, but the chinook had just blown in and there was no snow. Besides, would a pregnant woman be digging you out of snowdrifts? We hoped nobody would think too hard about it. They usually didn't. Anyway, those dudes in the ritzy houses would never think of clearing their own snow.

"Red, you said that there was some other breaking news."

"There was," he replied. "Louie called me and told me they had found a match for the fingerprints on the steering wheel of the car. If they did, it obviously means that this character had a criminal record and probably something serious."

"And his name?"

"He didn't say. That's why I'm meeting him tomorrow morning."

"We've got to find this guy and quickly," I said. "I suspect he has information that could be prejudicial to his health, or perhaps somebody else's.....even ours."

Red nodded and left. I sat there and hoped that Rita would not get any worse.

CHAPTER 6

When Rita woke the next morning, she was quite ill. Her leg was badly swollen. I didn't hear a peep from her for about half an hour. That was not like Rita at all. I offered to get an overnight bag ready for her visit, but the mysteries of what goes into these things were quite beyond me. Guys, you know what I mean. I go away for a week and can fit all my necessaries into my sports bag and still have room for a couple of presents on the way back. Rita was only going to be away for two days, three at tops. Her luggage was less like an overnight bag and more like an overnight trunk.

While Rita was full of optimism, she reminded me where her will was. I didn't need to know what was in it, but she stressed I would be expected to look after Artie. I complained it would be cruel and usual punishment.... for the bird. And possibly for me. That bird never stopped talking, and he always seemed to have it in for me. Drawn blood a few times. Please god, make sure to take care of Rita, I thought.

This talk of wills was all a bit pessimistic, and I tried to deflect the conversation. Rita decided that we would have to leave early to buy a new nightdress. I had plenty of pairs of pyjamas I'd never worn. But, oh no, we had to pop into the Bay, and it had to be something expensive. There were plenty of nice-ish pieces in the discontinued box, but she insisted on something more expensive. She told me that if she was to meet her maker, she wanted to be well dressed. I thought her maker might have more pressing issues on his mind than her nightdress. Then again, who was to say that her maker was a man? I began to see her point.

It was a quiet drive to the clinic, but to be honest, my mind was elsewhere. Both Louie and Jen had called, and I got the idea it was quite urgent. I could be a bit of an unthinking prick at times and ignore them. That would piss them off. But Rita was far more important, and I wasn't going to get distracted. I could ignore the calls for the time being.

The clinic ward was all they said it would be. Once we had signed in and been given a Covid mask embellished with the MMC logo, Rita was led to her room. It was beautifully appointed with every luxury imaginable, but I was one luxury they could do without. It was made clear that no visitors were to be allowed and there were to be no exceptions. I left with a bit of a heavy heart. We'd not been separated much before. I wandered down the corridor, followed by the nurse. As I did so, I noticed that the guy in the next room had a catheter inserted into his arm. The nurse realized I had seen this and quickly closed the door and ushered me out. He did not look at all well. I was glad that Rita had not noticed him.

I think you know where I went next. The coffee was always good in there and it gave me a chance to call the guys. I called Jen first. She had accepted the invitation to surveil the Connors' property and had been a couple of hundred metres away for much of the morning. There had been only one visitor to Mrs. Connors in the first few hours, as well as one person who knocked on the truck window and asked her to unblock his pipes. I wouldn't know how I would have dealt with this. It was probably quite innocent, but you never know these days. There are some weird buggers out there. Anyway, Jen was very professional in dealing with these sorts of things and told him to fuck off in a very erudite way.

Later in the morning, she said that she had spotted a BMW sports car drive into the grounds and seen a middle-aged, opulently dressed and long-haired man be greeted by Connors. She had no idea who he was, but she was sharp enough to jot down the car registration number. She immediately called Louie and asked him to check out who the owner was. It was not long before she had the answer. It was Lonnie Greene. Well. well. That Lonnie Greene.

Now many of you would not know Mr. Greene but if you were in the field of finance, you would know him very well. He used to have a radio show that loosely dealt with all things financial. He'd been very big in Vancouver and was probably second only in fame or infamy to the legendary Murray Pezim. Many assumed that he walked on the edge of criminality much of the time. Some had called him the Teflon man of Howe Street. I reckoned he had some powerful investors in the judiciary. He had recently moved to Toronto, where he was reported to be brokering some big deals, but was on temporary assignment back in Calgary.

What he had to do with Connors, we'd have to find out. Perhaps it was harmless. But I doubted he was collecting for orphaned kids overseas. The rich always seemed to mix with each other. But perhaps there was something to delve into. He had left her house after about an hour and had probably returned to one of the brokerage houses in Calgary. I told Jen to hang about for a couple of hours to see who else emerged and then drive into Bragg Creek and have a pleasant lunch on the firm.

If Jen's news was interesting, what Louie had to tell me was startling. They had identified the prints on the steering wheel as coming from a small-time crook called Jake Corman. He had a record of violence and had spent a few years in jail. Recently, it appeared as if he and his associates were being employed by rich businessmen for protection. These guys don't mess about. Officially, he was now doing odd jobs and some stunt work in theatre and movies. There was one thing for sure. He was a bad actor.

What better way to seal a deal than to add a bit of persuasion from Corman and associates? Or if you wanted to get rid of somebody that was excess to needs. Well, I wasn't prepared to go there yet. The question was what he was doing now and where could I find him? Why were his fingerprints in that car?

Louie was quick to point out there was no convincing evidence that Corman had actually driven the car up to the Forestry road. Perhaps there was a valid reason for his prints being on that steering wheel. Maybe he had driven the car before. There was only one way to get to the truth, and that was to find Corman. That was the problem. No one seemed to know where he was. There had been reports he had been hiding out in a house near Confederation Park on the north side of Calgary and Louie gave me the address, but that had to be confirmed. This man was keeping a low profile. The issue was why.

In a way, the events of the morning had given us some interesting clues, but interesting clues can dissolve in a nanosecond. We'd have to sit down and discuss our next move. I invited Red to meet me so that we could discuss what to do next. He wasn't very far away. I just had time for a sausage breakfast biscuit before he arrived. Thank god for all-day breakfasts. It was against my coronary diet restrictions, but I only had one a week. A life that's half as long and twice..... You probably know the saying. Red ordered a non-caffeinated tea without sugar. Jen was a Vegan. It would not be long before Red followed in her footsteps.

"So, big fella. What's the next move?" I said. "Find out more about Lonnie Greene or see if we can find Corman."

"I think it has to be Corman," Red replied. "If he had nothing to worry about, he wouldn't be lying low. That's the way these guys work."

"Do you think the police will try to find him?" I said.

"Doubt it. Louie told me that the case was essentially closed. So what if Corman's fingerprints were on the steering wheel? Suicide or death by natural causes was something that they likely wouldn't pursue."

"We have an address near Confederation Park," I replied. "We could do some reconnaissance and ask around the neighbourhood. Of course, it would help if we knew what he looked like. It might be on Facebook, but probably not on a Google Search."

"Come, come Sid. You don't think we thought about that."

"Red. You're a pro. One of the best. You have a reputation to uphold. A man of your talent would be right on this...well ninety-nine percent of the time."

"You're bullshitting me?" he said.

"I'm sort of bullshitting you, Red. But you are a pro. OK. Did you get a picture? Yes or no."

"Course, I did. I called Louie. He called the vehicle registration office. Played the heavy cop and voila, we had a copy of Corman's driving license."

"Let's have a look." Red passed me the xeroxed copy of the driving license. "Not exactly a looker, is he?" I said, though, to be fair, I had nothing to boast about.

"Yeah, the long thinning hair sliding down the back of his head and glasses can be a problem. If you cut the hair, ditch the glasses and he lost about twenty pounds, you'd never recognize him."

"Anything else?" I replied.

"Apparently, he's only about five foot five. Wears elevator shoes."

"You'd be surprised how many of these punks are short-arsed, overweight.........and liable to violence," I said.

"Must be some sort of compensatory psychological mechanism," said Red. "Small man syndrome and all that shit."

"I don't go for that psychological crap," I said. "Probably used to get beat up at school if he bothered to attend. Of course, it makes fuck all difference these days when you're facing a sawn-off shotgun."

"No point in saying put the gun down. I feel your pain. We can offer you counselling," said Red. He chuckled.

"Shall we send Jen out to do the surveillance?" I said. "She did a pretty good job in Bragg Creek, but she better be really careful this time."

"I agree, Sidney, but she's a smart cookie. She knows all the angles. I'll call her and ask, but I'm sure she'll say yes."

"Alright, let's say we've agreed on that."

"Let's leave her for a little while," Red said. "She's probably enjoying a nice lunch in Bragg Creek."

"Good thinking, young man. So, what do you think of this Greene guy? Know anything about him?"

"Look, I'm no expert on the corruption of high finance," he replied, "but I've heard that Greene can be pretty shady. He once put in for an NHL franchise until they realized he had nothing like the money needed. He was just a complete bullshitter. What do they say in business? Always use someone else's money. He might have changed now for all I know. You never know with these characters."

"Think we should do any more investigations into him, Red?"

"Possibly. Possibly not. There's no obvious connection to a crime. But we'll leave his name on the blotter."

"What the fuck is a blotter?" I said.

"Doesn't matter," said Red, rolling his eyes. "Let's just say notepad."

"Make sure you write it on a notepad. You know what my memory is like."

"What are you doing for the rest of the day?" said Red.

"Probably going home to take a rest, and then I'll pop in and see how Rita is doing this evening. Oh, and charge my cell phone. I'm nearly out of juice. And that's what I intended to do except I forgot to do it. What did I say about my memory?"

When I got down to the Clinic later that afternoon, I had quite forgotten that visiting wasn't encouraged. As I got into the reception area, I got a bit of the stink eye from the security guard who was manning the desk. I mean, he was decent enough. He said that Dr. Berryman had not left and would probably have a word with me. He called Berryman, who answered. The guard told me that Berryman would be right out.

I sat down on one of the plush chairs, but as I did so, my cell phone rang. The call display showed that it was Mrs. Connors. I assumed she was calling to void our contract. I hoped not. I'd spent a lot on Christmas, and I still had not deposited her cheque. I would do that on the way home.

"Lou Diamond Investigations. How might I help you?"

"Whom am I speaking to?" she said.

"Sydney Arbuckle," I replied.

"Mr. Arbuckle, I have some urgent news for you," she said. "I have decided to.........."

At that point, my cell battery died. No warning. I looked at the security officer and asked if I could use the Clinic phone. I told him it was urgent. As he pondered the request, I felt Dr. Berryman immediately behind me. As I turned, he nodded, and I dialled the number.

"Mrs. Connors, I apologize. My cell phone died. You were telling me that you had some urgent news for me."

"Look, I don't want to lie about this anymore," she said. "I know what happened to my father, and I think you should know."

"You found out what happened to your father. Do you want to tell me over the phone?" I said.

"It's a very complicated story, Mr. Arbuckle, and I'm not about to discuss it over the phone. Why don't you drive out to my place tomorrow afternoon, and I'll tell you the whole story?"

"Why don't you make a written statement?" I said. I thought that without it, it might be hearsay if I was asked about this later.

"That seems very reasonable. It might be a long document."

"No problem. Just make sure it's signed. I'll see you tomorrow afternoon. Would lunchtime work?"

"Yes, it would. I'll see you then." With that, she abruptly ended the call.

At that point, I noticed Dr. Berryman tapping his watch as if to say the phone call was over. It was. I fully expected to be billed for the call by the Clinic

"Mr. Arbuckle, we explicitly stated that there were to be no visitors," Berryman said. "But since you're here, I can confirm your wife's treatment has started. The first injections have been administered and she is feeling rather poorly. But that's what we expect in these situations. I've just talked to the nurse, and she tells me that your wife is sleeping soundly, and all the indications are very positive. Now, if you can make sure your cell phone battery is recharged, you are free to call us first thing in the morning. If you don't recharge it, I suppose you won't be getting through."

What a pumped-up prick. On another occasion, perhaps before my heart attack, I might've grabbed him around the collar or some other soft part of his anatomy and told him to fuck himself. Unfortunately, my intended was in his care and I didn't want to risk any payback. I politely thanked him and left the building. I quickly deposited Connors' cheque. I had plenty to think about that night. What was Mrs. Connors about to tell me?

CHAPTER 7

My sleep was fitful that night. I guessed that deep down I was worried about Rita's health. At one point, I thought about calling Red, but the news could wait until the morning. I made sure that my cell phone was charged.

The next morning, I got up, had an early breakfast (just add hot water), and called both Red and Louie. Louie was not available, so I left a message to tell him I had some urgent news and would visit Mrs. Connors that afternoon. Red was involved in another case, so I decided to go out to Bragg Creek on my own. It was likely that our involvement with Mrs. Connors might be about to end. I just had that feeling.

The roads on the way to Bragg Creek were completely clear of ice and snow. It's amazing what the Chinook winds will do. The Blackfoot people had called this wind the "Snow Eater" and it was easy to see why. The temperature could change up to thirty degrees in an hour.

I drove up to the mansion along muddied roads. I hoped I didn't get stuck. Mrs. Connors' car was parked outside. I wondered why she had not parked it in her quadruple garage.

When I walked up to the front door, I was puzzled. The front door was ajar. While the weather was very mild, I could not imagine why she had left the door open. I rang the doorbell but with no answer. You just don't want to walk in, though it hadn't stopped me before. But I realized that there might be a problem. I hoped not. I would probably have to go inside eventually. But first, I thought it might be wise to call her on her phone. No answer. I waited a couple of minutes and tried again. Still no answer. I walked in through the front door, took off my muddied runners, and called out her name, but there was no response. I checked out the lower floor of the house as well as the garage. There was no sign of her except for a half-eaten bowl of cornflakes and a barely touched cup of coffee. At this point, I began to get concerned. Breakfast should have been over several hours previous. I doubted Connors was a late riser.

My immediate alarm sensors began to vibrate when I noticed a trail of muddy footprints going up the ornate stairway in front of me. In a house that had been kept immaculate, this was particularly disturbing. Perhaps Connors was ill. I didn't want to consider any other alternatives, at least not yet.

I avoided the footprints very carefully and tried to keep my fingers off anything that would leave prints.

The footprints led up onto a balcony overlooking the hall below. I went to what appeared to be the main bedroom and pushed open the door, which was already half ajar. There was no sign of a body at first, but I could see the blood that was staining the floor and in places had pooled. I walked round to the other side of the bed and there was her body. Although I was no expert in these things, it looked as if she had been strangled and then stabbed in the chest multiple times. The murderer was not taking any chances of her surviving and she hadn't. In her struggle, it seemed as if she had grasped one of the curtains which had fallen on the floor. It was soaked in blood. Some of it had partly dried, which suggested that the death had not been recent. There was no sign of a murder weapon, though I didn't hang around to look. There was an open safe in the corner of the bedroom. It looked as if it had been rifled through. There were open jewelry boxes with some of the contents littered over the floor. I quickly stepped back and ran downstairs. I reached for my phone and called the police.

I probably should not have done this, but I poured myself a glass of whiskey from the liquor cabinet downstairs and then ran out to my car. As I did so, I realized that Connors' office had been rifled as well. Often, these were indications that someone wanted you to believe the motivation was a robbery. And sometimes that was the motivation, but I didn't buy it. Why had the jewelry not been taken from upstairs? I doubted it was cheap costume jewelry. I called the cops again. It might take them a while to get out here.

I didn't want to stay in this house a second longer. As a police officer, I'd seen death on many occasions, but despite what some people say, you never really get used to it. The whiskey hardly helped, but I wasn't going back in for another one. I still have the occasional bad dream about these sorts of situations.

I moved my car away from in front of the house and then sat in my car and called Red. and then Louie. He told me to stay where I was. It was inevitable that I would have to stay around to answer a few questions from the police. Right now, I might be considered a serious suspect, though God knows what the motivation could have been. As a cop, you always want to talk to the person who finds the body.

It took the police about 20 minutes to get there. They asked for my description of what had happened and, more to the point, what I was doing there. I said that Connors had contacted me regarding a possible investigation. The fact that I had called Louie before they arrived seemed to impress them. Louie arrived a few minutes later.

I knew the game only too well. Remember, I had once been a policeman. Until they found another suspect, I was probably it. Not that the cops were unsympathetic. At least, I did not get the hard-core grilling that others often had to undergo sometimes from me. They asked me to sit in my car.

As I was sitting there in the car, one of the detectives strolled over to me after about fifteen minutes. As he approached, I heard him say to a colleague that they had found some evidence that they would have to check out. It was likely that the intruder had been driving a vehicle with bald tires and a heavy oil leak. They had found this evidence just outside the front door. I didn't want to rain on their parade, but that could only be my car. I was more than surprised that it still had some oil.

After about half an hour, and probably on Louie's word, they decided to let me go. I would have to attend an interview the next morning at the police station. I drove back down into Bragg Creek and went into the only bar still open. A double whiskey seemed the best bet. I thought I had given up alcohol years before, but there was a time for everything. That was two whiskeys in a couple of hours. As I sat there, I saw a couple of ambulances pass by. The police would still be there for several hours. I finished my whiskey, topped up my oil, and left town.

I arrived home just after lunch. Red and Jen were already there. They already knew what had happened, and they had more questions than answers. I didn't expect to hear from Louie, at least not just yet. But I did. He told me to keep my chin up, and he thought I might want to know who she had called in the previous 24 hours and who had called her. He could get his balls in a vice for this if he was found out, so I would have to keep quiet about it.

Later that afternoon, he called me back. There wasn't much information. It seemed as if she had called me and then shortly after that the Clinic. She must have been trying to reconnect with me and hadn't realized that it was not my phone. There was a spam call from the Canada Revenue Agency. I mean, everybody got them. And then there was a call from an unidentified phone. Almost certainly one of those phones that you bought from a convenience store that hid your identity. Not the sort of call that you would expect Connors to get. She had also called Lonnie Greene. That probably related to the meeting they had had the day before. Apart from a couple of advertising calls, that was it. We would have to wait to find out what was on her computer.

We sat there and drank hot chocolate with whipped cream in the later afternoon. There was a big storm brewing, and the temperatures were expected to plummet again. I remembered there was a sign on the Alberta border that said 'The chance for snow is never zero.' Never a truer word.

I avoided the world that evening. Red and Jen hung around. It just seemed to be the thing to do. Stress can hit you hard. I put on my battery-heated slippers and put a TV dinner in the oven. Jen was aghast. But as I pointed out, it contained all the essentials. Carbohydrates, protein, fat, and enough preservatives to keep it fresh for a few years. All I needed was something to preserve me for a few more years.

Before we started our discussion about the case, I thought I should see if I could contact Rita or at least get an update on her condition. I was able to get through to the head nurse right away. She told me that Rita had a restless night but was now doing much better. She thought that she might have to spend an extra day at the clinic, but they would know tomorrow. I told her to let Rita know I had called. I didn't mention that I might be the chief suspect in an ongoing murder case. That wouldn't help her health one little bit.

We had very few clues to go on. Jen had done surveillance at a residence near Confederation Park and had even knocked on the door without luck. She did buttonhole the next-door neighbor who did not know Corman but said a well-muscled bald guy had been there last week. Perhaps that was Corman. He drove a green Ford pickup, which we found out was registered to him, but he had not been seen by anybody for a while.

The more important question, we had to focus on, was who had killed Connors and, more importantly, why. We first carefully went over my conversation the night before. It was probable that Connors knew the story of her father, Kevin Sykes. She knew all about his demise and it was obvious that she wanted to keep it secret, at least until she had talked to me. The problem was somebody else had become privy to this information, and this had probably been her death sentence. That's my theory and theories are meant to be disproved. It would be me who would start the ball rolling.

"O.K team. Any other ideas?" I said. Not being democratic here. I just didn't have a clue.

"We have evidence that Corman was possibly involved in dumping Sykes's body," said Jen.

"Yeah, but pretty weak evidence," I replied.

"True. But it is possible that Connors found out and was going to somehow shop him," said Jen. "But note I said possibly twice."

"Not a bad idea," said Red, "but part of it doesn't make sense."

"What part of it?" I said.

"Red's quite right," said Jen." If Connors had something on Corman, she would hardly call him up and admit it and we can't even be sure that she actually knew Corman"

"That's a good point," I replied. "Jumping to conclusions is a dangerous strategy in this game. A more thorough examination of her phone records might tell us more," I replied.

"Any other observations, boss?" said Jen.

"There was no evidence of forced entry. So, you might suppose that Connors probably knew her killer. The security in that place was excellent."

"It's a good point," said Red. "I know that area. It's a bit isolated. People often lock their doors. You have no idea who might be out there."

"If she had spotted a stranger on the security camera she would probably not have let him in. My money is that she probably knew her killer and let him in without second thoughts."

"Anything else?" Jen said.

"Well, the killer was obviously looking for something."

"What do you mean?" she replied.

"The safe in her bedroom was open. There were valuables, such as jewelry, left in there. I suspect this was not costume jewelry. As I was leaving, I noticed that her office had been ransacked. The intruder must have been searching for something. It was a real mess though, to

be frank, not much different from my office. Anyway, if we knew what
he was looking for, we'd be nearer to the truth."

"You said he," said Jen. "Who knows? It might have been a woman."

"With that amount of violence?"

"Now that is sexist," she said.

"There's a saying that hell hath no fury like a woman scorned,"
said Red. He was right. Women were quite capable of the most violent
crimes and when I was a cop, I'd been involved in a few of them. But
they were usually crimes of passion.

"I've been on the receiving end of that type of scorn a few times,
but I somehow survived, when stuff was thrown at me," I said. I
laughed, though it was probably not the right emotion.

"You're not suggesting she was having an affair?" Jen replied.

"Not exactly. She was in her late fifties," I said.

"I sometimes give up on you, Sid," she said. "What has age got to
do with it?"

"Alright, it might have been a love affair gone wrong," I said

"Or she might have been seriously let down in a business deal.
She might have decided to get her own back, and it cost her," Red
suggested.

"A sort of you've fucked me. Watch this, buddy. I'm going to fuck
you."

"Not quite in those words. But you get the general drift," Red
replied.

"She was obviously important in the business world, but what's
the connection between her father and the business world?" I said.

"Could it have been this Greene character?" replied Jen

"Possible," I said, "but it could have been anybody. The fact that
Greene had just seen her means absolutely nothing."

"Should we continue the investigation, Sid?" said Red.

"I think we should. We've been paid very well for the next two
weeks. I'm not going to welch on our obligations to Mrs. Connors.

There are ethics in this business," I replied. Sometimes they are well hidden, I thought to myself.

"Fair enough," said Red."I guess we have two weeks to solve this whole mess."

It was as we were discussing the situation and about to refill our cups that I received a call from Louie. In any investigation, you can expect times when you go three forward and two back. This was eleven back. Louie told me that the security system at the house had been deactivated. That was a bugger. That could have told us everything. And sometimes that minus eleven can go back to a plus two.

Louie had some interesting information, not that he was going to admit to having made this call. This case was still in the hands of the police and if found out, he could have his balls cut off. But Louie was always a guy who led with his dick, and it hadn't been cut off yet.

The forensic folks had been on the job and thought they might have a lead. There was some tissue underneath Connors' fingernails. She must have put up a hell of a struggle. It was likely that the murderer had scratches on his face. They were going to send their samples away for DNA analysis to see if they could find a match. Nothing was certain, but occasionally this type of thing came up trumps. The only problem was that unlike the cop shows you see on the box, DNA analysis doesn't come up with answers within a day or two. It can take weeks and often doesn't help at all. However, that was not the best news. There was something better. Louie told me that there was a message to me on Connors' computer. He read it out to me. This is what it said.

"Mr. Arbuckle, I have to apologize to you. I lied to you about the life insurance. It was taken out for a different reason than I stated. I'm not proud of it. I'm telling you this to set the record straight. The world of big business can be an ugly place and people can do ugly things to you. I know that I won't be popular, and you can expect all the usual denials. I'm going to name names. ....'

Except she never did. It was probably half-finished when she met her demise. But it seemed to back up our theory that somebody had definitely pissed her off and she wanted to get even. It might have something to do with big business, but what and who? This might get Corman off the hook.

I told Louie to keep in touch whenever possible. He informed me that if I hadn't heard from the police, I soon would be. He was right. Ten minutes later, just as Red and Jen were leaving, the inevitable call came in. The police informed me they wanted to interview me at ten the following morning. There was no need to retain a lawyer, at least not yet. I hoped it would be routine.

The following morning, I received a call shortly after breakfast telling me that Rita was ready to come home. I called her on her cell to let her know that I would be a bit late. I told her about Connors' murder and mentioned that the police were interviewing an important suspect. I didn't tell her it was me. Didn't want her to have a relapse.

When I got down to the central police station downtown, I was a few minutes late. My Chevy refused to start. It looked like the end of that car. It was 17 years old, and it had finally given up the ghost. I decided to go on the LRT. It was either that or borrowing Rita's Smart Car. I knew she would not be impressed if I tried to squeeze her into that car to bring her home. I decided I would take a cab from the police station to pick her up, always assuming that they let me go.

The interview was predictable. I had done a few of these before when I was a cop. Two detectives in a plain white room with a two-way screen and a hidden microphone. One the good guy, one the bad guy. You see it every night on true crime shows. And it is true. I didn't know these two guys. The force was getting younger by the year. I apologized for being late. They looked at each other and asked me if my car leaked oil and had bald tires. I had to admit that it did. They looked at each other and started laughing. Not quite what I was expecting.

They asked me to recount the events of the night. I told them exactly what had happened and there were a few questions. I told them we were involved in an investigation and that I'd told Louie that I was going to see Connors. They nodded. They had talked to him already. I hoped that it was not for a bollocking. And then they asked me a very odd question. They asked to see my boots and to confirm that I took a size 14 shoe. I did and on inspection, I knew they believed me.

Let me tell you about my feet. Call it a genetic abnormality, but you wouldn't imagine that I had such big feet. I say feet, but my right foot was a 14 and my left a size 13. You might consider that to be not that unusual, but I do have to tell you that I used to be five foot eight. With age, I have shrunk to five foot six. You rarely see small runts like me with such big feet. There is the rumour that the size of one's feet correlated precisely with the size of....... well, you know what I'm talking about. I can tell you it simply isn't true. I would never deny the rumour when I was in the dating game, but that seems so long ago now.

I mean, they didn't have to tell me this, but I wondered why they were asking about my feet. I'm glad they didn't ask me to take my socks off. I had forgotten to change them that week. They did eventually tell me why they wanted to know about my feet and once I understood their motives; I knew I was no longer a suspect. They told me there were two sets of footprints on the front steps of the house. There was a much smaller footprint with a much larger one on top of that. That was mine, but I could see why they thought the smaller one might be mine.

The interview didn't last much longer. They asked me if I knew anyone who might have had it in for Connors. I had some ideas, but they were based on what Louie had told me, and I wasn't going to let him down by mentioning that. We shook hands, and they told me that if I came up with anything, to let them know. From the way the interview went, it looked as if the killer had not driven up the muddy path but had probably walked up the grassy verge at the side of the path. Only my tire marks were evident. Smart move by the killer. This sounded like a professional hit.

I left the police station and hailed a cab. Before it arrived, I began to look through the front pages of the morning paper. It was only then that I realized that I had picked up the paper from the police station. I could imagine the headlines the following morning. Ex-cop cleared of murder is now charged with petty larceny. It was a funny old world. You could never rule anything out.

I got into the cab a few minutes later. The driver was from Afghanistan. I always enjoyed talking to these guys from other places. Let's face it, we all came from other places. I shocked him when I told him I could tell him something about Afghanistan that he didn't know.

"What's that?" he said.

"Afghanistan has a cricket team."

"Fuck you, mate. I used to be the captain of the team," he said. Cricket was universal in the rest of the world, as was the fuck word.

I complimented him on his English skills, and moments later, we arrived at the clinic. I gave him a good tip, at least for me.

Rita was waiting for me in the clinic waiting room. It was nice to see her. It was not nice to see Dr. Berryman. Did I mention I thought he was a supercilious prick? Still, I thought I'd better behave myself.

"Mr. Arbuckle, as you can see, your intended is looking very well." Why the fuck did he have to say that again? Common-law husband would have sounded better.

"Yes, I see that. So, thank you Dr. Berryman, and your wonderful staff. Now I suppose we can piss off." I mean, I didn't intend to say that. It just sort of slipped out.

"No, no, before you go, I should let you know that we have written a cheque out to your good lady. I am sure she will spend it wisely." This guy didn't know Rita. "There is one other thing to give you."

"What's that?" I said.

"As you know, our organization is so grateful for your involvement that we would like to provide you with a unique investment opportunity."

Now, I wasn't born yesterday. I had bought too many penny stocks on the Vancouver Exchange to know a promoter when I met one.

"I don't have much time at the moment," I said. "Perhaps another time."

"Not to worry," he replied. "I've talked to Rita about it and there's a brochure and agreement in the package of information. I'm sure you'll be impressed."

With that, I picked up her baggage and led her out of the building. Fortunately, there was a taxi waiting outside. We jumped in. It reeked of marijuana. I started to get hunger pangs. Just before we reached home, I suggested that we'd better deposit the cheque. You never knew with these characters.

When we got home, Rita was all for starting to clean the house. I put my foot down about this. She should just take it easy and then do it all tomorrow. She told me that any blood clots and swelling had disappeared. Which was good because these things can kill you. The whole thing had gone off without a hitch, though she pointed out that the guy in the next room had not been so lucky. That must have been the fellow I had seen with a catheter in his arm. He wasn't there the next morning. When she asked about him, she was told that the information was confidential and could not be released. She thought the outcome had not been good.

Rita was far more impressed with Dr. Berryman's offer to make us investors. Did I mention Berryman was good-looking and wore a Rolex? If you like that sort of thing. I think that Rita was enamoured by the thought of having a stockbroker. It was the sort of thing you could mention at cocktail parties, not that we ever attended them. But if that's what she wanted to do; I would go along with it.

There was to be an information session at the Brockbank Stockbroker House three days later. This was described as a boutique securities dealer. What the fuck did that mean? Probably meant they had a nice brochure and an even nicer reception area. I didn't give a shit about that sort of stuff. I've done a lot of successful deals out of the back of a truck. Of course, many of those were illegal, but who was to say this wasn't? The brochure showed cocktails would be served at 3:00 p.m. and that formal dress would be appreciated. That was going to be slightly difficult for me. Sure, I'd just had my three-piece mohair dry-cleaned, but it was my feet that would be the problem. Shoe stores don't often sell size 14. The only footwear I had was my cowboy boots. I had my runners, but they were still caked with mood from my Bragg Creek visit. They probably wouldn't be appreciated. I opted for the boots.

Rita was quite excited about the whole thing and phoned to confirm our attendance. It was then she told me that there would be a guest speaker who was going to give a presentation. His name was Lonnie Greene. We knew all about him, but almost certainly not enough. There was a brief bio of this guy. He had been so successful at one time the business had given him the title of Mr. Gold. Rita was impressed. Did I say that Lonnie was a good-looking, middle-aged dude with an expensive suit? Rita would be absolutely no match for this guy.

CHAPTER 8

There was no doubt that Rita was much better. The treatment seemed to have worked. She was full of beans and had nothing but good words for the Clinic. She also had suddenly become interested in the stock market. There is a saying out there that if your barber talks stocks, it's the time to sell. Since Rita cut what was left of my hair, I was not in a position to say one way or the other. But Rita's enthusiasm began to rub off on Jen and I heard them talking about stocks for the next few days. And the MMC corporation was all they could talk about. They had done plenty of medical research in the previous few hours. The two of them now knew who the chief players were, how many shares the company had, and all the analyst ratings. MMC was a vast conglomerate, but MMC Canada was an offshoot of the world organization. That's not to say they had not had some success. They had reported that they had come up with a drug for Covid, a revolutionary treatment for hemorrhoids and their latest innovation was the anti-clot drug which they expected would revolutionize medicine. I had just read a report on the internet about blood clots and vaccines. So, this shit had come along at the right time. At least that's what the brochures said.

With regard to the ongoing investigation, we needed an infusion of ideas. Jen had been looking for Corman but had no luck. The problem was she couldn't do it full-time. She could easily have missed him and it was not yet a top priority. Perhaps he had flown the coop. But if he had, there would be people searching for him, but not by us for the moment. All we could do was speculate. It would be a long shot to conclude that he was her toy boy. Most murders involve sex and money, but I wasn't buying that in this case, at least from the sex angle. Of course, it was a police matter now and all we could do was provide an assist. Louie still kept in touch where he could, but there was only so much that he could tell us.

Because I think she needed a bit of support, Rita managed to get Jen an invitation to the cocktail event. She knew a lot more about financial issues than we ever could. The meeting was to be held in a room at the Westin Hotel in downtown Calgary and was only for the invited. Of course, if you had a lot of money I assume you could easily get invited in the blink of an eye. I'm glad we had the official invite. Without one, the girls might have got in. I doubt I would have got past the front door without one.

Dress was described as semi-formal, but I saw nothing wrong with wearing a string tie with my suit for the event, but Rita did. She suggested...no demanded ....that I put a sweater on. Whatever she desired, I thought, but I was under the impression that they were trying to impress us, not the other way round. I knew my work cowboy boots might not be appreciated, but so what? I could have passed for a local rancher, which was not a bad thing. Many of those lads were loaded. At one time, they owned half the city and probably still own half the province.

Jen offered to drive us downtown. My car was being read its last rites and the Smart Car would not fit the two of us. Hell, it was a bit of a squeeze for one, if that one was Rita. Please don't tell her I said that. So, we arrived in Jen's new Audi. Jen let me drive. Thank god, it was automatic and not a stick shift. Nice smell of leather in the car, but you can get that with an air freshener. The way I looked at it, any car could have got us there with leather seats or without. I was not one for style. I was big on respect, though. As the girls got out, the doorman told them to inform their chauffeur that there was free parking at the back. He pointed at me. If I'd been on my own, I would have given him the sign. Instead, I waited for them to get out of earshot and told him I had a message for him. It had to do with sex and travel. He got the message.

The girls waited for me in the lobby. I thought we all looked quite smart in our matching LDI masks. If you haven't worked it out, that stood for Lou Diamond Investigations. I mean, some people might have thought that it stood for London Dominion Investments but, of course, it didn't. That was Rita's idea. She thought it would make a good advertising strategy. It didn't. I still have two big boxes of masks in my basement. Call me if you want one or even a hundred.

The girls first went to the bathroom. Have you noticed how women always go to the bathroom together? Could you imagine what Louie would say to me if I said, "Heh Louie, I'm going for a crap? Why don't you come with me? Bye, girls."

A few minutes later, we made our way to the meeting room and were allocated a seat. Because of the Covid thing, there was the necessary social distancing, so the room seemed sparsely populated. Once we were seated, they gave us what looked like a souvenir program. The girls seemed to be more interested in what the other women were wearing. For that matter, most of the guys were as well. The old boy in front of me, who almost certainly was a rancher, seemed to be on the point of falling asleep. It was hot in this room. I knew it would not be long before the finger food and non-alcoholic wine appeared. The girls pretended it was lovely, but I was not one to appreciate sardines and gorgonzola on tiny bits of toast.

After about ten minutes, the meeting started. The initial comments were made by Berryman, who detailed the successes of the company. There were a lot of pictures of laboratory technicians with test tubes and pictures of equipment. Probably stock photos. The laboratory technicians were, of course, hot babes. If they were males, they tended to have pimples and look as if they were permanently worried. Then came what was supposed to be the highlight of the meeting. The one, the only, Lonnie Greene, rose to speak. This guy certainly looked the part with his dark black hair, which he wore in a bun, but Botox and hair colouring could only achieve so much. He was one of those guys with an obvious gut but who was able to hide it with expertly cut trousers. I could never find them in Walmart. He seemed to be fixated on the blond hostess's tits right in front of him. Or perhaps she had his speech printed on her chest.

His talk was quite impressive, with lots of slides that seemed to say the same thing. Radishon was an amazing new drug. The stock price was seeing a parabolic rise and financially, things had gone extremely well for the company. I must admit, it was a very polished presentation until Greene started to talk about the equity markets. He had just said that some people were expecting the markets to blow off when the old boy, who was now fast asleep, farted. Not a silent one but certainly deadly. I mean, everyone heard it. That was a real blow-off. Some people started to snigger, but I'll give Greene credit. He merely pointed out that all medications seem to have some side effects. I was just grateful we were following social distancing.

The key to the meeting was the special offer that was to be made to people who had taken part in the trial and their families. I don't quite remember the term, but they could buy options or warrants. This would enable them to purchase shares at a discount price later on. Sounded good to me, but what if the stock price was lower than what you paid for the options or warrants? Not a question that anyone was going to ask, of course, because everybody pretended that couldn't possibly happen.

The rest of the presentation was devoted to questions. There would only be time for a couple. That was always suspicious to me. Don't want anyone to ask a troublesome question, do you? Inevitably, someone asked how successful the trial had been. Had there been any problems observed? None at all, really, was the answer. Approximately two percent of the subjects had experienced slight adverse reactions and were dropped from the trial. They said this was because of pre-existing conditions, but I thought everyone had a pre-existing condition.

That was why they were doing the trial. No one seemed to pick up on this. Most of them had dollar signs in their eyes. There was just time for one more question. Somebody asked where all the patients had come from. Greene answered that physicians and hospitals provided them. Because of the Covid situation, they had gleaned some of their patients from the drop-in centres, so long as they were otherwise healthy. He then joked that some of these people could really use the money. I was not amused. Of course, his company probably needed the money a bit more than the poor unfortunates in drop-in centres. They didn't hold these meetings because they were nice guys.

Berryman indicated everybody would be followed up at three and six months. They did not expect any problems. At that point, Greene excused himself and said that he had another urgent meeting to attend at 4:30. I assumed it was with the leggy blonde who was waiting by the door, and he left with her arms around his waist. This guy was certainly attracted to blondes as well as money.

We didn't hang around after the meeting, though we thought of popping into the Owls Nest, a fancy bar in the hotel. Not a good idea. Jen and I, at least officially, didn't drink, and Rita was restricted because of the medication she was on. We went straight home. It was starting to snow again. What do they say? If you don't like the weather in Calgary, just wait ten minutes.

We sat at home talking about the deal. Rita was very bullish about getting involved, but Jen was less enthusiastic. When they asked me what I thought, I suggested we should be cautious. A fool and his money are easily parted. I admit that comment got me into a bit of trouble. I wasn't suggesting that Rita was a fool. Not at all, but it took a lot of backtracking on my part to get back on the right side of her which was usually the front.

If doing the deal was what Rita wanted, I'd go with it. But I thought we should investigate the company a bit more thoroughly. We started by looking at the brochures provided to us. The company brochure was impressive, and Berryman's vita was especially impressive. He had more degrees and affiliations than I could possibly recount. The company had certainly done a lot of research and published it widely. That meant nominations for various awards. He noted that he only listed his major publications. There were so many others. Much the same as me. I only referred to my one major publication, 'How to safely conduct surveillance in public toilets.' You might laugh, but it was published anonymously in Criminal Affairs Today. I can send you a print if you are really interested.

MMC seemed to be a company worth billions of dollars, though perhaps not the Canadian arm. It was only worth a couple of hundred million. I suggested it might be wise to Google the company name. If there was dirt on the company, that was just the way to find it. There was some dirt. There had to be. Most pharmaceutical companies have faced more than a few lawsuits in recent years. I mean, someone once told me you weren't a real businessman unless you'd been sued. Given recent evidence, these guys were very real businessmen. Most of the lawsuits were about the adverse effects of some of their other drugs. They'd paid out a lot of moolah to sort this out. The press rarely reported on the issues or if they did, it was on the bottom of the back page. Hell, some of these companies were probably providing grants to the ailing media. That's the best way to get good publicity.

We were about to log out when I noticed one significant piece of information that you might ordinarily have missed. One clinic in Toronto was called the Connors Clinic. It had to be her. That was probably why she had been seeing Greene the day before. She was probably a significant part of the operation, and this was confirmed when we discovered she was a significant shareholder. I have a fertile mind. Perhaps she had quit the company and was threatening to sell her holdings, and this rattled a few cages. And perhaps......No, I just had a fertile mind. The real issue was what the hell did this have to do with her father?

We went ahead with the investment, but we would have to go through Jen's broker. It would cost about four thousand dollars. Darn,

I could have bought a good vehicle for that. Not much of one to be sure, but I had contacts in the business. Most of them were semi-honest. Of course, if we went through Jen and we made some money, we'd have to pay her the capital gains. If the shares went tits up, she could have the capital loss.

It felt as if it had been a long day. That was certainly the case for Rita. Perhaps it was the excitement of the meeting. Perhaps it was the effects of the medications she was on. We agreed that she should lie down for a while. I discussed with Jen what we should do next. She was still up for looking for Corman, as were the police, but I wondered if she could help us in another way. Apparently, her broker was a bit of a financial sleuth. Would it be possible to do some investigation into Connors, but more especially Greene? She told me she was doing some design work for her broker for free, so she had a bit of leverage. It might tell us nothing, but it might tell us a lot. I just had a bad feeling about Greene. I knew from his reputation that he was one of the pump-and-dump types of promoter. That means they hype the stock up and get as many suckers in as possible and then sell it before people realize there is a problem. They are not usually caught. I hoped that Jen's broker could provide some insights.

I was just getting ready to leave our house to pick up some cannabis from the strip mall opposite when Louie arrived. He told us that Corman's trail had gone cold, but they expected to find him. He also told us they had examined some surveillance tape from another house near Connors' and had seen a green truck parked in the roadway outside the Connors mansion, followed a few hours later by a rusting piece of shit. Louie howled with laughter. I thought he was going to choke. There are plenty of green trucks out there, but as I said before, there are no coincidences in crime. It meant one thing, though. My rusting piece of shite might be used as evidence. Better keep it for the time being.

I wasn't going to worry about anything else that night. It was Rita time. I made her sit down and suggested that I would prepare a decent meal. There are some good Hungry Man's out there and even I couldn't fuck that up. I even joined her in watching her favourite cooking show. It was called 'Cook-off.' Clever name that. It featured some foul-mouthed Aussie bloke. It was a competition where the losers were told to cook off when they lost, and they immediately cooked off. The show was all a bit weird to me. There were all sorts of odd dishes suggested. Who could imagine you could do that with oysters and chicken feet? I just hoped Rita didn't try. And then Red called to see how Rita was doing. He was involved in another case, but he agreed to do a bit of surveillance on Lonnie Greene. It was a short conversation. Not sure what he would look for, but I am sure he had some ideas. I had a lot on my plate the next morning. I had to find a decent car for less than five grand. At least I didn't have to do the washing up.

CHAPTER 9

Our profits for the year were way up. I could have afforded a BMW or Merc. Alright, a second-hand one. At worst, a leased one. But why? Anything too fancy was ostentatious. You park a Maserati down the street, and everybody notices it. And then, in some areas, they'd nick it. No, I wanted something that wouldn't stand out. So, I went down to Johnny's Autos in Dover. We had rebranded it as Johnny's Rotten Autos. He was a good bloke for a crook. He knew I could have put him away several times in the past, so he would always give me a good deal. I chose an old dark green-blue truck. I mean, the back was rusting badly, but the tires were good, the clock had not been rewound that much and it had a decent heater. Johnny told me it ran good. I asked Johnny to stencil "Imperial Exterminators" on the side and we would have a deal. I'd pick it up the next day. I just hoped there wasn't another company with the same name.

When I got home that morning, Red and Jen were just arriving. Jen was doing some teaching that day. She did some virtual teaching now because of the ongoing restrictions. This girl was still an expert at pole dancing and she'd be doing some demonstrations online. She had an interesting piece of news. One of her students was the chief nurse at the MMC clinic. I thought it might be useful if they could get together for coffee. Now, I'm not saying there was anything suspicious about the Clinic but if there were I would want to know and right now.

Rita was on another of her health kicks that day. No coffee. We were all offered organic tea. I didn't know you could have inorganic tea but, to be fair, it was pretty good. When I told the guys about my new truck, the reaction was indifference or amusement on Jen's part. She was amused by the Imperial Exterminator bit. She wondered if we were planning to exterminate the royal family. Red thought it would not prompt any undue interest at all and would be a great surveillance vehicle. Of course, little Miss Cynical, and by that, I mean Jen, thought it would not go well in the ritzy neighbourhoods. What were we trying to exterminate? It definitely wasn't rats. Alberta didn't have any.

Once Jen had left, Red and I discussed what we might do from now on. We decided that for now, the police could look after Corman. We both decided that it might be worth taking a longer look at Greene. I suppose our mandate was to uncover what had happened to Sykes and why it had happened. Mrs. Connors had paid us handsomely for that, and the check had cleared. We could have moved on to other things, but once you get involved in a case, it's hard to put it down.

Red left to do some research on Greene and perhaps do a bit of surveillance. We'd have to find out where he lived, but that should be easy. Remember, we also had a contact via Jen to look into some of his financial dealings. It was going to be a straightforward day and then I got the phone call. It was from Louie. I mean, his news would not typically have raised an eyebrow, but someone else had been found dead in his car. He was frozen solid as well. Foul play was not considered, according to the cops, but they said it couldn't be ruled out. Since there had now been two of these incidents, I concluded that it definitely couldn't be ruled out. What the fuck was going on here?

The body had been found in a car that was parked on a minor road in a valley near the Last Chance Saloon in Wayne, about two hours east of Calgary. Not the sort of place you would want to visit in winter. It was close to Drumheller.

If Drumheller is a bit of a quirky place, Wayne is one of the Badlands quirkiest places. It's situated up a valley about 14 km south of Drumheller. There used to be coal mines in the area. It's just off the main highway and you have to cross eleven one-way bridges to get there. While the Saloon is closed in the winter, in the summer hundreds of Harley-Davidson riders meet there for the Wayne Rally. I suppose you could call it the ultimate biker bar.

The car had been found about 500 yards from there. It seemed to have been parked there for at least three or four days, and possibly longer. It was well below freezing and there was a biting north wind. The chinook that warmed Calgary rarely made it out this far. Louie suggested we meet out there. It was about 90 km east of Calgary and normally I wouldn't have thought twice about it. But remember, I didn't have a car for that sort of terrain. The snow would often blow off the prairies, drift across the roads, and make life very difficult. I would have to rely on Rita's Smart Car. I made it to Drumheller but only just. I got stuck a couple of times, but Albertans are a helpful lot. You might have to wait a few minutes, but someone would always stop to give you a push.

When I got to Wayne, the cops were attempting to extract the body from the car. I should point out this was not a local police effort. The RCMP were involved. Although Louie, who was technically off duty, had no mandate here, he knew most of the blokes out there. Let's just say he was an interested observer, and the RCMP did not object to his involvement.

There were so many similarities with the Sykes situation. The car was stolen. It was an Uber vehicle that had been stolen in Calgary a few days before. There was a suicide note on the front seat. The typically vague 'my life is complete shit' type of note. It was unsigned and could have been written by anyone. And there was an open bottle of pills on the front seat. There was also a badge that looked like it was an old Hell's Angel insignia. It would appear that the person or persons involved assumed that the City Police and the RCMP would not be swapping notes. How wrong they were.

It took over an hour to extract the body and then an ambulance picked it up. There was not much to be done. It would take a few days to thaw it out. The vehicle was then towed away by the RCMP. We assumed that the corpse and the car would be sent to Calgary. That was where the car was from and where the most sophisticated forensic services were available. I knew Louie would liaise with the local RCMP, so I would be kept in the picture. Unofficially, of course. I followed Louie back into Drumheller before the snow closed the road.

Drumheller wasn't a bad place if you liked an enormous plastic dinosaur on the edge of town. But to be fair, it was the home to the Royal Tyrrell Museum. This housed one of the world's largest displays of dinosaurs and was Canada's only museum dedicated exclusively to the science of paleontology. And it had a Tims. In we went and sat there with cups of steaming coffee. It was just beginning to go dark but in the middle of winter it never really got very light in this place. Drumheller was in a deep valley and when the sun was low in the middle of winter, you never really saw the sun. I suspect the pharmacies sell a lot of Vitamin D capsules at this time of year.

We sat there for a few minutes and talked about the situation. How likely was it that there would be two apparent suicides with a generic suicide note, both within a couple of weeks? It simply made little sense, but it must have made sense to someone. We didn't hang around for long. There were snow squalls expected from a cold front that was due to blow through overnight, and you didn't want to get caught on the highway into Calgary.

Louie left just before me. I needed the bathroom. Coffee will do that to me. When I came out, I noticed a green truck just pulling away opposite. It had a heart shape on the front door. I couldn't see the driver. It could have been Corman's truck, but I was betting that there were quite a few old green trucks in Alberta. I jumped into the Smart Car and began to give chase. It was a losing proposition. As I drove up the hill towards the Horseshoe Canyon turnoff, I gradually lost ground. The traction was very poor. Seconds later, the truck disappeared into the distance. If it had been Corman, what the fuck was he doing out here? I could only speculate. The only thing certain was that it might be a difficult drive home. I'm glad that for once, I had charged my cell phone.

It was when I walked into the house two hours later, I realized I'd screwed up. I had promised to pick up some medications for Rita that afternoon. She couldn't do it herself, of course. I was driving her car. If it had not been for Jen, I would have been facing the silent treatment for a few days. You guys know what I mean. 'How you doing, honey?' 'Oh, I'm fine,' said with a long face. Usually lasts three days, but it once lasted six weeks for me. Can't they develop a vaccine for this sort of thing?

Jen had picked up Rita's pills from the clinic and, in doing so, had made an important contact. The chief nurse, her student, was on duty and they had agreed to meet the next day. Nothing was said, but Jen definitely got the impression that there was some discontent at the clinic. It might have to do with the egotistical Berryman. I wouldn't work with him, but it could be something else. Not that all was bad. I checked the internet when I walked in and lo-and-behold, the stock price for MMC was up nearly fifteen percent. We were making a profit, at least on paper. That would lift Rita's spirits a bit. And there was an announcement that new clinics were to open in Edmonton and Vancouver. Things were looking good for the company.

I offered to take care of supper that evening. I told Rita that she could have anything she wanted. Anything! She said she wanted curried prawns. Not a problem I said. Just take a nap for half an hour. I'll look after it. Off she went. I put on an apron and then called 'Skip the Dishes.'

We had an excellent dinner. Of course, she realized I hadn't done it. I had once tried to make fried rice for her. It didn't dawn on me you had to boil the rice first.

It was shortly after dinner that Louie called. He told me that the Uber vehicle was registered to a guy in Confederation Park. Where had I heard that name before?

The body in Wayne had not been completely frozen. It was estimated that the body had been out there for only about three days. There was no sign of violence, whatsoever, and there was no indication of the body's identity, except for one thing. The body had a ring on which was engraved with 'From Lucy 2010.' It wouldn't easily identify this person, but it was a start. Must have been five thousand Lucys in Calgary and we couldn't interview them all. There were also a couple of pill bottles on the front seat. They seemed to be out of date. There was also the suicide note. Louie noted something quite unusual about the notes from the first and second suicides. They had been printed on the same rather fancy paper. It had a watermark which said 'Basildon Bond'. I had no idea who this guy was. A rather odd name. It could have been James Bond's brother, Basildon. I tried to find him on the internet. This was not the name of anyone. It was the name of a UK company. It was described as the most trusted name in personal stationery, and it had been in operation for the past 100 years. So, what the fuck was this all about? I'd never seen this sort of paper in Canada, but then again, I never wrote letters with a real pen. Actually, I never wrote letters with anything.

I didn't expect Red to turn up that night, but he still thought Jen was with us. I think it was just an excuse to let us know he had come up with something significant. Apparently, Mrs. Connors was about to make a further huge investment in MMC, but insiders told Red that the deal had turned sour and she was about to dump her stock in the organization. Just as we'd speculated. There was no reason identified, but the dumping of stock and the negative ramifications of this could have been disastrous for the company. That couldn't have been allowed to happen. That was perhaps why Greene had met with Connors 24 hours before she died. This is not to say that Greene himself was involved in murder. But you couldn't completely rule that out either. And we still didn't know how Kevin Sykes was involved in this.

Somebody else could have been very upset about what was happening and took things into their own hands. Perhaps it was another major investor. Red was going to continue his investigation and, according to him, he had some new sources to talk to over the next few days that would clarify the whole situation. We still had the six days for which Connors had paid us. We would do our best to help solve this situation before our contract ran out.

CHAPTER 10

Once Red involved himself in anything it was a hundred percent or nothing. The next morning, convinced that Greene was up to some mischief, he decided to surveil him. I'm not sure what he hoped to find, but I wasn't going to stop him. I'm big on initiative and certainly didn't want to discourage him.

Since it was the weekend, Greene probably would not be at work. He lived out in the Bel-Aire section of Calgary. It might not be the most elite part of town, but it was darn close. At the same time, Jen had arranged to meet with her colleague from the clinic. I had focused, along with Louie, on finding out who the deceased man was. Because the body had not been too disfigured, we managed to get a photo of him we might use in identification. Since there was no documentation in the car, it might be a long process, but we were able to identify the Uber driver. My first option was to call him, but there was no answer. I would try an in-person visit. He lived in the North West of the city.

My new vehicle was to be unleashed on the unsuspecting public after lunch, so I had a bit of time to get there. I drove over in Rita's little car. The Uber driver had no idea when his vehicle was stolen until last night. He had been away for a few days and when he got back, it was gone. He had left it in his driveway and, according to his neighbour, it had been gone for a couple of days. The police and RCMP had contacted him and told him that the car would be returned later that afternoon. There was no damage, though he realized later that whoever stole it was into heavy metal. There was a CD in the player.

That wouldn't help us at all unless the cops had dusted it for prints. Besides that, he couldn't help us very much. He didn't know the Uber driver from the first incident and said that he had never heard of Sykes. I left my card with him so that if he remembered anything, he could call me.

Then I went home and took a cab out to Johnny's in Manchester. The police had informed me that there was no need now to keep hold of my old beater. I certainly couldn't disagree with that.

If you looked at Johnny's from the street, it looked like a fly-by-night operation, and I suppose it was. When I was with the cops, I'd put him away for six months for fraud. Look, he was just a small-time businessman who bent the rules a bit. There were people in the business towers in downtown Calgary who bent the rules a lot more and they got away with it. Some seemed untouchable. Money, bribery, the right lodge. Who knows? Anyway, he'd polished up the truck a bit and covered some of the more obvious rust spots. He thought I might get another thirty thousand kilometres out of it. That was fine by me. But one of Johnny's problems. He was dyslexic. He couldn't spell worth a damn. I'd asked him to put ' Imperial Exterminators' on the side. Instead, he had put 'Imperial Ex-terminators' on the side. What did he think we were? A bunch of pensioned-off hitmen driving around in an old green truck. Oh, well, it would have to do. I drove it home carefully. I didn't want to waste any miles more than necessary on this baby.

When I got home, there was a message from Jen. She had met with her friend from the Clinic and she had a slightly different perspective on the situation. Her friend was not happy with the management. She thought Berryman was a prick, so her judgment could not have been that bad. She was concerned that the results were not what the press releases were suggesting. Several people did well on the drug trial and some did not. The results might not have been quite as successful as reported. Hyperbole and obfuscation could cover up a lot. Red's words. Not mine.

Jen suggested she was going to discuss the results with a statistician friend of hers. It was reported that the company was going to present its results at a conference the following Sunday in Banff. This was to be for invited guests, mainly doctors. You know the game. Free board and lodging for the weekend, free samples of our drug, and then keep on prescribing it, thank you very much. Despite not having an invite, Jen was intent on attending and taking her statistician friend with her. I should add that there was also a virtual presentation because of Covid but Jen realized that any of their questions could easily be ignored on Zoom. She would always find a way to get in. I didn't want to curb her enthusiasm, but the links to our case were getting a bit tenuous.

It was only after I had talked to Jen that I realized I had other domestic duties to look after. I had quite forgotten that it was New Year's Eve. We had invited Jen, Red and Louie if he could make it. I was also to invite the deaf guy next door. I pinned a note on his door and asked him to come over at eight. I then went out in my new limo and picked up a few goodies for the evening. I didn't want Rita to do anything unnecessary. After all, she was still convalescing. I picked up some alcohol for a New Year's toast. I thought about picking up some non-alcoholic wine for Jen, but I had no idea what she liked. Wine to me was red or white, sparkling or flat. I knew Louie would bring his liquid flame thrower. I hoped he wouldn't suggest that we drink it at the stroke of midnight.

Before we met socially, I called Red to see if he had come up with anything. He had very little to report except he had noticed a green Ford pickup visit briefly at Greene's house. Holy shit, I hadn't told Red that was what Corman drove. Then again, the green pickup could have been mine except, of course, it wasn't. There must be a few of those vehicles around. He also mentioned that he had been in touch with Louie. They were getting close to identifying the latest suicide. There was a possibility they would either identify him using fingerprints or dental records. Since it was New Year's Eve, any results would not come for a couple of days.

Jen and Red arrived that night on time and were followed by Arnold, our next-door neighbour. He had little in the way of speech, probably because he was deaf, but he was able to communicate with a portable device that he carried around with him. And he was a good-looking dude for his age. I'm no expert on that sort of thing, but I just took Rita's word for it. He was a bit of a silver fox. Longish silver hair and a nicely trimmed beard and was he built. He would have looked good in my three-piece mohair suit. Rita said he exuded class, something which she'd never been able to say about me. Well, I had class. It was somewhere below second.

As we introduced ourselves, he pointed to his device and typed something in. It said, "Do you know any signs?" I only knew one, and I didn't think that would be appropriate. But one way or another, we managed to communicate. There is always the idea that the deaf are limited in their abilities. Boy, was I in for a surprise? This guy seemed to be a genius. He wrote computer programs, was a wizard with encryption, and had made a fortune on the stock market. The sort of guy who could tell you when a market was rigged. And he could lip read. We asked him about his family. He had two sons who were living overseas. We asked him about his wife. He turned on his device and typed in, "She was from down under."

"Oh," said Rita. "She was from Australia?" He typed in. "She was from hell." Even Rita pissed herself laughing at that comment.

We all got along famously. I was glad I had asked him over. His deafness was not a hindrance at all. And then Louie arrived. I knew he was a bit tipsy, though Louie never showed you he was drunk. I just knew from experience. He just became louder and started waving his arms around a lot. After a few minutes, Arnold typed something into his device.

"What the fuck is wrong with this guy? He's fucking noisy, isn't he" I laughed. He laughed. Louie had no fucking idea what it was all about, and we weren't about to tell him. But there was one issue. How the hell was Arnold going to lip-read Louie? We weren't deaf, but we always had trouble understanding what he was saying. But it was not a problem for Arnold. Perhaps it was his accent that usually defeated us, but, of course, Arnold couldn't hear the accent. He relied on lip-reading. He seemed to understand Louie very well. We might have found a translator. Anyway, Louie just kept drinking his tuica. He offered Arnold a glass. He accepted and then asked for another. We knew Arnold was deaf. At this rate, he might be blind.

After downing a few eats, we decided we would get the Scrabble board out again. We decided on three teams. I would play with Rita, Red would partner with Jen, and we decided Arnold would partner with Louie. It was obvious that Red and Jen would win. My money was on Louie and Arnold to finish second. Inevitably, Rita and I would finish last, but I decided on a variation that would give us a chance. If you could use a dirty word, you would get triple points. The real issue was to decide what a dirty word was. So, we decided that you would have to use it in a sentence. Now I'm not sure that Jen was particularly impressed with this. She rarely swore at the worst of times. When Red used the word 'pussy', she used the following sentence. "My pussy cat loved to drink cream." We objected it was not dirty. She replied that nobody said the sentence had to be dirty, and she was right. It might come as no surprise that, for the first time in recent history, Rita and I won the game. Louie inevitably objected, but we had no idea whether the words he used were dirty or even words. And that was it for Louie. He had one more glass of tuica and within moments, he was snoring. We guided him downstairs into the spare bedroom. He was in no state to go anywhere that night.

We waited for the inevitable New Year's countdown on the screen, but things had changed with Covid. It was now a virtual countdown. Still, we got the idea and launched into Auld Lang Syne, except Arnold did it with sign language. After the obligatory handshakes, we were ready to halt proceedings for the night when Jen's cell phone rang. I think we all assumed that it was a friend calling to wish her a happy new year. I mean, who would call at that time of night? It wasn't a friend. After a few moments, Jen's demeanour changed. "Go fuck yourself, buddy," she said and halted the call. I'd never heard her swear before, and certainly not like that.

"What the hell was that all about?" I said.

"A threat. This guy told me to stop messing around with things that didn't concern me. If I didn't, there could be big trouble in the new year. And I mean big trouble."

"You didn't recognize the voice?" Red said. He looked pissed.

"No. But I'd recognize it again. I guess I've been asking just too many questions of the wrong people."

"From our perspective, it might be the right people. Any idea what the number was?" I said.

Jen checked her phone.

"It was private. Could have come from anywhere. Probably one of those phones you can use for a month."

"How many people know your phone number?" I said.

"That's a good point," she answered. "I don't give my number to just anyone."

"I think it might be an idea if you checked who you have phoned in the last little while. That might give you a clue," I said.

"It's probably bullshit," said Red. He'd calmed down a bit. "I've had a few of these calls myself. Sometimes it's nothing more than teenagers taking the piss. They think this is just amusing. I think that's the motive here, but I think we should be very careful."

With that, they decided to go home. The call had extinguished the festive spirit. They'd have to be careful driving home. A lot of drunks out on New Year's Eve and a lot of sober people who were just poor drivers. We agreed to meet in a couple of days to see what progress we might have made.

At that point, I thought Arnold would leave, but he was still halfway through a glass of tuica. He knew something was amiss because of the phone call, and he was determined to find out. Because he could lip-read, we slowly told him about the case. What harm could he do? We told him about all the details of what had happened and all the possible clues. He told us he thought he might be able to help. He had a few skills that we didn't have, skills that might surprise us.

Arnold certainly seemed to have a lot of technical experience. He said that he couldn't promise, but he might be able to work out where Jen's call had come from if he could get hold of her phone. More importantly, he asked if we could get copies of the suicide notes that the dead victims had left. He said the police might be missing something. What he didn't say was what they might have missed, but he seemed to have a theory. He also said he would check out MMC and see if there was something unusual about its trading patterns. He didn't exactly tell us how he could work this out. It was something to do with statistical analysis. When we asked him if he had that sort of experience, he told us he used to work for the Toronto Stock Exchange to look for this sort of thing. Who hadn't he worked for? I thought he might have other connections, but perhaps I just had a vivid imagination.

I was impressed that he could do so much with statistics. It was all completely beyond me. I couldn't even spell statistics. It was a fascinating one-sided conversation. He certainly knew his statistics and how they might show some malfeasance on behalf of the company. I should add that malfeasance was not a word I knew until this week. I had seen it on my Word of the Day calendar a couple of weeks back.

Arnold was a really interesting guy and to think we had sort of ignored him for a couple of years. Sure, we had occasionally waved, and I had held my tongue when his dog pissed on our lawn. Of course, if we had told him to piss off, he wouldn't have heard us anyway. I wondered if his dog could respond to sign language.

This guy had the talents that could be useful to us. We could even use him for surveillance duties. I mean, who the fuck would question an old deaf guy who couldn't speak? I looked at Rita. She knew what I was thinking. She nodded. I asked Arnold if he was interested in becoming part of the organization, if only temporarily. He didn't say 'yes'. He didn't say 'no.' There was a beaming smile. I knew he was onside. We couldn't pay him much at first and I think he understood this. It was a case of paying by results. And so, Lou Diamond and Associates gained one more associate. Mr. Arnold Townsend.

The next morning, we got up late on New Year's Day. It was sort of tradition for us. Another part of the tradition was our New Year's Day walk up Nose Hill. The weather was sunny and very cold, which was just the sort of day for a brisk walk. A few dozen people thought the same thing.

Nose Hill is one of the biggest urban parks in Canada and it overlooks the city, which is to the south. While the wildlife is now limited, the views from the top certainly aren't. You can see over the foothills to the Rocky Mountains to the west, over 100 kilometres away. Unfortunately, there was no sign of a chinook over the mountains this day.

When we left for our walk, Louie was just stirring. He must have had a hangover, but he would never let you know. He was on duty in a couple of hours. That probably wouldn't be a problem for him. We told him we would call him later in the day. I wondered if he was fit to drive.

We managed to find a parking spot near the Calgary Winter Club. It was one of the oldest winter clubs in Calgary. It was not the sort of place I would have joined. First, I probably would not have been asked. Wrong pedigree and all that. To be fair, I had heard nothing but excellent things about the place. Second, you would have to show a semblance of fitness to be involved. I certainly had nothing close to a semblance. I assume they would have considered me a medical risk.

We didn't go very fast, in part, because it was uphill, and the ground was icy in places. We didn't think about going more than a couple of kilometres and we didn't. It gave us time to talk about the case. In reality, it was me who did the talking and Rita who did the listening. We had been paid for another five days, but I had the feeling that we might extend this on our own coin. A good investigator just doesn't stop when the money runs out.

When we got to the parking lot, we saw it. It was there in plain sight. A green Ford pickup. It certainly seemed to match the description of Corman's vehicle, but I couldn't be sure. There were so many of these green trucks about that I had never noticed. It might be Corman. I couldn't remember the plate number, but I got my flip-top phone out and took a few photographs. There was one thing for sure. If it was Corman's, he was a scruffy S.O.B. The inside of the truck seemed to be littered with crap. Of course, it would have been completely hypocritical of me to say any more. I mean, I wasn't a complete slob. I changed my air freshener every couple of months.

The issue, of course, was what the fuck was he doing up there, if it was him? If he was still living in Confederation Park, that was just down the hill. I couldn't imagine that he was there for the fresh air. Perhaps he had just dumped the vehicle and abandoned it. Remember, the police were looking for it. When we got home, a few minutes later, we contacted Louie, and he told us the cops would send someone out there as soon as they could spare someone. After all, it was New Year's Day and there was only limited staffing.

The rest of the day was spent peacefully, but we had one more social event that night. We weren't really theatregoers, but Red and Jen had given us tickets for a show that was being put on by the Calgary Pro Arte Theatre Group. This was a new group whose mandate was to put on virtual theatre. The Covid situation had meant that traditional theatre was, to all intents and purposes, completely fucked. So, this group streamed some of their productions. Tonight's show was a murder mystery called 'The Butler Didn't Do It.'

You watched the play, looked for clues, and could send in questions to be asked of the cast. Red thought this would be a great challenge for us. We thought Arnold might be interested. Well, we didn't want to be embarrassed. We texted him and fortunately, he agreed to join us. Thank god. We didn't want to look stupid to the theatregoers of

Calgary. It might be bad for our business. We were in for one surprise, though. The Pro Arte Group had several sponsors and there were two names we knew very well.

I had been to a few murder mysteries before. I'll be overly nice about them. They were usually crap. A third-rate meal at a restaurant and a playlet filled with actors who thought their job was to be funny. Most of them were quite unsuccessful. This was different. It was professionally performed and the story, though unrealistic, made some logical sense. Essentially, there were two murders. In both cases, the bad guy had replaced the innocent pills in the doctor's bag with some poison. And Voila. Two very dead people. Course, Rita and I had no idea that the bad guy had used sleight of hand to swap the pills. Needless to say, Arnold spotted it right away. We won free tickets for their next performance. He was going to be a great addition to the team. It was only as I lay in bed that night that something important crossed my mind.

CHAPTER 11

I had just gotten out of bed, the next day, when Louie called. The police, with the help of the RCMP, had come up with some news. They had lifted some prints from the Uber vehicle. They would compare them with their database. More importantly, they had managed to identify the body using dental records. Not many people would have recognized Jake Sharples, and few could have been aware that he had disappeared. He didn't have a permanent residence and had spent some time in local hostels. It emerged that he had been ill for a time and had been quite depressed because of it. In fact, some witnesses said that he had been suicidal for a few years. It was not a surprise to them when it was suggested that he must have committed suicide. But this clearly made little sense. The problem was that he did not appear to have a driving license. So why would someone who couldn't drive, steal a car in Calgary and finish up in Drumheller to commit suicide? Unfortunately, this did not appear to bother the police, and they wrapped up both cases as being suicides. We'd been down this road before. I decided it was time to get the team together to discuss what was going on and this time I would invite Arnold to join us.

For once, everybody arrived on time. I explained why we had invited Arnold to join us. I had to do this very carefully and slowly. Remember, Arnold could only lip-read. Rita explained she was proud of my diction. I wasn't quite sure what she meant by that, but I let it pass. I was able to describe Arnold's considerable technological background as best as I could. Everybody seemed to be impressed and after a few handshakes, we got on with the meeting.

I started the ball rolling with a review of the situation, starting with the inconsistencies of the two suicides. It simply made little sense. Red wondered if the two cars had been returned to their owners. If so, could we inspect them? Louie answered those questions.

"Yes, friends. Cars back with owners, though I suspect being used now on a daily basis."

"That isn't very helpful," Red said. "Any evidence other than the fingerprints has probably long gone."

I suddenly noticed Arnold trying to attract my attention. He was furiously inputting on his tablet. He passed the device to me. On his device he had typed, "Did both cars have GPS?" I repeated his question to the team.

"Since it was an Uber car, I would expect that those things were mandatory," said Red.

"You're right," said Louie. "They did have them." Jen did a mock clap.

"Fucking right on," said a voice somewhere in the room. We looked around. Holy shit, it was Artie, the parrot. Now I must admit it was none too clear, but that is what it sounded like. Everyone howled with laughter. I had to explain what the parrot had said to Arnold. He couldn't lip-read the parrot.

"So, why is that so important?" I asked. Arnold furiously typed on his device. "Because I might be able to see where the cars had been before they were dumped." I read this out to the group.

"That's brilliant Arnold," I replied. Everyone nodded. "This could give us some very important information." I was tempted to ask Arnold how he could possibly work this all out. I decided not to. It really didn't matter. We probably wouldn't be able to understand, anyway.

"Any more thoughts on the threat from the other night?' said Rita

Jen answered. "We think it was probably complete bullshit. But you have to be concerned about it."

"How did they know Jen's number?, added Red. "The problem I have is that she hasn't really been that involved in this case. She's done a bit of surveillance and asked a few questions, but that's about it. So, it may have nothing to do with this case at all."

"She had that meeting with the chief nurse at the clinic," I said. "And I'm sure she asked some pointed questions. That might have got back to somebody, but who and why would they be upset" "

"Possibly by accident," said Jen. "There was nothing unusual about our meeting. Now to be fair, my friend had some grave doubts about the clinical trial, and she wasn't hesitant to voice her concerns."

"Where did you meet?" I asked.

"We were going to go out for coffee, but she was busy. We settled for coffee in the Clinic's lounge."

"You may have been overheard," I said.

"Possibly," she replied. "But the links between the Clinic and Sykes and the latest victim are still slight and possibly non-existent. Remember that."

"Are you going to follow it up, Jen?" I said.

"I am. There is a paper presentation at the Banff Centre in a couple of days to announce the final results of the trial. It apparently is the last chance to convince the world that their drug is the next best thing since penicillin."

Arnold tapped away at his device. "Or Viox," he typed.

He didn't have to explain. I was on that shit for a couple of years. It was supposed to help with my arthritic pain, but there were suspicions that it had actually caused my heart problems. The lawsuit had cost the drug company billions in damages. Not a problem. They'd just increase the price of their antacid tablets. The government would look the other way.

"You going on your own?" I asked. "Don't you think you should take someone with you, given the threats?"

"Don't worry," she replied. "I have an expert in statistics going with me. If there is something that makes little sense, she'll spot it."

"And she is?" I asked.

"My next-door neighbour Chandra. She works in biomedical research at the University or used to. She is an Emeritus professor now. Won't get anything past her. She's been stuck at home because of the Covid crisis and is bored shitless. We can do a nice early lunch in Banff and watch dusk set over the town after the conference."

I heard Arnold clattering away on his device.

"Want me to come? I won't say much."

I read this out to the group, and we all laughed. Arnold laughed as well.

"Just keep in touch, Jen," I said. "We want you to stay safe. Any more news about Corman, Louie?"

"Nothing yet, though that was his vehicle up by Nose Hill. The police think it's been dumped. They said they'd keep watch over it from time to time. The boys still think he's in town. Apparently, he has a really bad history. Let's say investigations are ongoing."

"You going to follow up with a bit more investigation of this chap? Perhaps some surveillance of that address in Confederation Park?" I asked.

"Yeah, I could do that," she said. "Just make a few inquiries. We don't know for sure that he lives there, but it's worth checking out. You never know. And what about you, Sid?"

"Well, I do have a line of inquiry that I'll be looking at. I won't say anything else. If I'm wrong, you'll take the piss out of me."

"Have it your way," said Rita. "When did you worry about what people thought? Of course, If you're right we'll hear soon enough."

"Anything else to talk about?" I said.

"Have picture of latest deceased," said Louie. "Want to see it?"

I took a look.

"Shit, he wasn't completely frozen like the other one," I said.

"Nah, he very cold but not frozen. He look quite peaceful to me."

He handed the picture around. It prompted little comment until it reached Rita. She pored over it quizzically. She handed it back to Louie.

"Hold on a minute," she said. "I've seen that guy somewhere before. Where was it? It'll come to me, eventually."

"Don't think too hard about it," I said. Now I was trying to be nice. Sometimes the harder you think about these sorts of things, the worse it gets. Rita gave me the one-finger salute. I decided it was time to adjourn the meeting.

"Is there anything else to talk about?" I said. "If not, let's break up for now and talk tomorrow. Oh, and if we could talk for a moment, Arnold." That was insensitive and prompted some slight discomfort. Of course, Arnold couldn't talk, but he just smiled and nodded. I am sure he heard worse. The others disappeared.

Once they had gone, I asked Arnold if there was anything that he had missed mentioning. He nodded. and began furiously typing. He asked whether he could get hold of the two typewritten notes that the two suicides had left. I thought that might be possible. If the police were deeming this a suicide, it was possible Louie could get hold of them or at least a copy of them. Why he wanted to look at them, I could only guess. I decided not to guess.

The one thing I wanted to know was where Arnold had learned all his skills. Perhaps he was bullshitting me. I had to be blunt with him. I asked who he had worked for. Secret, he mouthed. But I wasn't going to give up. I pushed him hard. Eventually, he started typing. I wasn't really prepared for the answer. In a sense, he didn't give me an answer. Just a few clues. I could fill in the rest. It had happened to me twice before in my life. In the space of two weeks several years back, I'd had the same conversation with two people who I had seen as friends, and they still are. One admitted to being from the CIA and the second who was English asked me if I knew what Military Intelligence was. Of course, I did. He meant MI5. They both stressed they were not involved anymore, but I called bullshit on this. Once in, you never leave. They can always call you back. And if somebody pushes you, just provide vague answers. That was the way the conversation with Arnold went. He didn't exactly admit it, but he never exactly denied it. So, he had worked for an organization with three letters. I just hoped that he worked for the good guys. Apart from that, I didn't give a shit. What he was involved in was none of my business. But I did start to wonder if he was actually deaf, but he'd heard Rita sing without complaining, so it was fairly obvious he was.

The conversation didn't go much beyond this. I told him I would contact Louie right away to see if he could come up with the goods. I was able to reach Louie about an hour later and he said he could get photocopies of the two suicide notes to me within a couple of hours. He told me to make sure that there was paper in the fax machine. There usually wasn't. I told Arnold I would bring them over once I had received them.

I had only just ended the call with Louie when he called back. I assumed he had pocket-dialled me but he was persistent and eventually, I answered it. He might have had a good reason to be calling, and he did. He informed me that the DNA analysis had come back. They identified Corman as the probable killer. The big issue was why he'd done this. I guessed that this had been done on behalf of someone else. There was some evidence that Connors might have known Corman, but probably only superficially. With her social status, he was not the sort of person she'd mix with. Probably no woman scorned there.

The afternoon gave me a bit of time for reflection. The police seemed to have made little progress in solving Connors' murder and even less in finding Corman. Was there a significant connection to Greene and could even Berryman be involved? My mind was spinning.

I knew we would need a major break in the case and two hours later, perhaps there was. This game was feast or famine. The two photocopies arrived, and I took them over to Arnold's. I knocked on his door. I had never been to his house before. I really didn't know what to expect. He had seemed so organized but like many brilliant people, his house was a clutter of books and papers. I say many brilliant people, but not all. I'm a long way from being brilliant, but I too am clinically untidy, and I tend to leave half-eaten sandwiches on my desk for a couple of weeks at a time. My view of all of this is that if I can eventually find something, why waste time being organized? I handed the papers over and Arnold indicated he would see what he could do.

I had no idea what Arnold could do, but two hours later, I found out. At first, it didn't seem like much, but he was able to tell me that the two letters had come from the same printer, but that was not all. They had been printed on a Winfried Laser printer. Now, I had never heard of a Winfried printer, but if we found one, we might have an idea where the two letters had come from. Two possibilities surfaced. We could see if a local distributor could give us any insights and, with luck, to whom he might have sold such a printer. Nice idea. That didn't work. The printer was only distributed in the USA. The only other option was to go searching for the printer. Once we found it, could we identify it as the one that had produced the letters? That seemed like a needle in a haystack idea, but Arnold thought he could find it. How the fuck he could do this? God only knows. I was a born-again atheist, so god was not going to give me any clues.

Although we thought about it, we decided that we couldn't just put out an advert in the paper to find out who had the printer. If you had been up to mischief, you would hardly respond. We would have to decide who might have one of these printers and search for it. This sounded like a credit card job to me. Lest you get the wrong idea, the credit card was not for buying anything. A credit card job in the business means a break-in job. You can get through most door locks using only a credit card. The issue was who was most likely to have this printer and whose house or office we would be breaking into. There were a few thousand offices out there.

One thing for sure was that the two dead men almost certainly did not have this printer. One other thing for sure was that breaking into anywhere could be a dangerous game. We would have to tread carefully. Getting caught might be perilous. And we couldn't expect any support from Louie. We could only count on the kindness of Louie and the cops for so long. I tossed and turned most of the night and as dawn broke, I reached a conclusion.

CHAPTER 12

There are some days when you are working as a private dick that you simply need to have a quiet day. When nothing seems to be happening there is always something happening underneath the surface. I could have sworn there was a car surveilling our house. I knew the signs. I also knew that it was easy to get paranoid and reach the wrong conclusions. The problem was that I had been spooked by the threat to Jen. But why would they be surveilling me? I decided it was just a case of paranoia.

Now I don't normally read the newspaper or even listen to the news. It's all depressing. We don't have a paper delivered but this day Rita picked one up in the tanning salon. I mean, I don't go for that tanning shit, but if it keeps the little-ish lady happy, so be it. I used to look at the sports pages but since sports sort of disappeared with Covid, I now go straight to the crime pages, and by that, I mean the financial pages. Gold was up for the second month in a row. That was good for me. I'd only have to empty my teeth to be a rich man. But there was something else, and it was plastered across the front page. There was a story about MMC. The report said that this should be one of the biggest private offerings in Canada, in the last ten years, and it was likely to close within the next few days. It all looked like peaches and cream and, to be fair, the stock price had doubled over the last week. My teeth would be safe for another year.

It was the end of the story that raised my eyebrows. There was an interesting article, albeit on the back page. The chairman of the company, Sir Miles Garrett, did not have a pristine background. He had been in charge of at least two companies before MMC that had been successfully sued in class action lawsuits. When I researched this, I discovered that his companies had produced a couple of drugs that purportedly reduced blood cholesterol. While they may have done that, they also had the habit of permanently lowering blood cholesterol. Several patients had died. There were, of course, a litany of denials and excuses. One couldn't let that sort of thing impede a big private offering. But it certainly might have impacted some investors if there had been more significant publicity. The bottom of the last page was not likely to do this.

I wondered if the author of the article, Ted Bourne, would be going to the meeting in Banff. Ted was a good guy. Used to play darts with him and so I decided to call him. Bourne had done several exposes of drug companies in the past, and I wondered if that was what he was focusing on. It wasn't. He was just glad to be doing any story at the moment. These were not halcyon days for journalists. But he was interested in the Banff meeting. If there was a problem and a possible big story, he would want to be the first to report it. I arranged to meet him the next day. I offered to drive him to Banff. He didn't have a car. Something to do with global warming. There had been fuck all evidence of that in Calgary for the last month.

I also had to call Jen and tell her I would meet her and Chandra, the statistics wizard, for lunch in Banff shortly before the meeting. We wanted to impress her so the Golden Arches would be out.

Other than that, it had been a rather quiet day. But in this business, you just have to wait five minutes and there will be a change. The change came in the form of Louie. He said that Corman had been spotted up on Nose Hill by walkers. They thought he looked suspicious, though they did not say why they thought that. Some people would probably find me suspicious. The issue was, why the fuck would Corman be up on Nose Hill? Killers don't usually go for a constitutional walk in the middle of the day. I doubt he was particularly worried about doing ten thousand steps a day. Perhaps it was a mistaken identity, but then again, perhaps it wasn't.

I then received a call from Red. He had been surveilling Corman's house for most of the day. He'd even talked to the neighbours who confirmed that he lived there, but they hadn't seen him in days. I decided that perhaps later that afternoon, I might get my credit card out and take a look at Mr. Corman's abode. Red was all for it. He was still worried about the threat to Jen's well-being, so for him, the idea was pretty much in play.

Before I left, Arnold e-mailed me. He had been able to work out that both the Uber cars had spent some time near Confederation Park. Now there was a coincidence. That's exactly where I was headed.

One thing that you have to consider when entering someone else's property is a cover story. If you are caught, it simply has to be believable. I remember in my early days. I turned up with a white stick and pretended I was blind. I broke into this guy's house, but on the way out, the next-door neighbour accosted me. I told him I was a blind piano tuner, and he believed me until I got into my truck and drove away. Rather spoiled the illusion, and he did call the police.

After consultation with Red, my cover story was that I was a Covid inspector. The city had designated several hundred people, or should I say spies, to find out if you were having illegal social gatherings, illegal because of Covid. People had bought the whole Covid shtick, so they'd probably cower in fear if they challenged me. I prepared myself a City of Calgary badge and a couple of official-looking forms and went off to meet Red at a local pub. Technically, we should not have been able to do this since, under the new restrictions that had come in the day before, at least for Calgary, we had to come from the same household. I was willing to say that Red was my gay live-in lover. I mean, in this world where a fart is discriminatory, who was likely to argue?

We weren't bothered and sat down to discuss what we might look for. That's always a good plan, but more often than not, it's the stuff you're not looking for that gives you the key information. We certainly had to check to see if the Winfried 2000 printer was in there. It would also be useful to see what was on his computer. What messages had he been receiving and from whom? And that was about it. But there's always something in these situations that you're not expecting.

We drove down to Confederation Park and parked Red's car just down the road from Corman's house. Unfortunately, his next-door neighbour, a Sikh gentleman, was in the process of clearing the sidewalk outside his house. Not a problem. In such situations, you face the problem head-on. I went up to him and introduced myself. I told him we were worried about social distancing violations and that we would have to check into Mr. Corman's house. There were three cars in front of his house. The poor bugger obviously had a bit of a guilty conscience because he left me alone rather quickly and disappeared into his house. He didn't notice that I was wearing my Lou Diamond face mask.

Breaking into the house was a piece of cake. Many of the old bungalows had fairly rudimentary locks. Probably borne of the days in early Calgary where there was little need to lock your front door. Nobody seemed to be watching, and there were certainly no obvious security cameras. Once inside, we went straight to an office-like area to the side of the front door. There was a computer and an older printer. Holy shit. It was a Winfried 2000 laser. My lucky day. I had fallen on my feet.

I quickly turned the machine on and printed a test sheet. But I was sure there was more to find. In the desk drawer, I found something that I had seen before. Several pill bottles with the CPTG designation on them. I took one and pocketed it. I also looked at a notepad. There was a note that said, "Call Berryman before lunch". Well, well, well. What was the link between Dr. Berryman and Corman? If I could work that out, I would be more than halfway to breaking the case. I went out into the kitchen and looked out of the window. There were several turbaned 'family members' leaving the house next door and scurrying down the back alleyway. I was tempted to open the window and tell them to get their arses back in the house, but I didn't want to blow my cover.

I then went downstairs and found a bedroom down there with a padlock on the door. Perhaps it was an S and M dungeon, but perhaps it was a temporary holding cell. Perhaps he just didn't want his sleep disturbed. I was not about to break the lock to find out. Before I left, I called Red up to see if he had any more ideas. He mentioned the hard drive, but I'd already checked that out. He also asked about any USB sticks. Brilliant idea. There was one inserted into the computer. I put it in my pocket and with that, I left.

The guy next door was back out, sweeping the pathway. I wagged my finger at him and told him that "keeping apart is keeping us together". I thought he was going to shit himself. Perhaps he was, but by then, I was back in the car. I knew for sure the guy wouldn't be calling the city to complain.

We left straight away with our bounty. Alright, it was only a memory stick, but that could tell us plenty. We decided we would first drive over to Red's to discuss what this all meant. Given the threats, Red did not want to be away from home for too long and I completely understood. The only problem about going to Red's was that I would have to put up with that coffee that goes into those tiny cups. It was all in the line of duty, I suppose. I could put up with it for once. Finding the printer was key. I mean the Winfried 2000 was a piece of crap. It was probably twenty years old, but it had a tale to tell.

I immediately texted Arnold and told him that I would be bringing over the test sheet when I got home. At the very least, this definitely tied Corman into both alleged suicides. The other intriguing find was the reference to Berryman. What the hell would he be doing dealing with a shithead like Corman? Although I hadn't taken the original note, I took the notepad sheet underneath. You've seen it on TV. Get a pencil and rub the paper underneath and there it is.

Then there was the issue of the pill bottles. Obviously, they were used to convince the police that the suicides had overdosed but which pharmacy had prescribed them. Remember, they were several years out of date. The issue was which pharmacy had filled the prescription. We decided to see if we could trace CHPG pharmacies. There was nothing even close in Calgary or the rest of Canada for that matter. I suppose it was possible that the pharmacy had closed down, but that seemed unlikely. Pharmacies rarely go bust. The pharmaceutical companies see to that. They need people to sell their drugs. For the time being, it would have to remain a mystery.

The USB proved to be a bit of a disappointment, at least at first. We plugged it into Red's computer but there was apparently nothing on it, or so it seemed. Now I'm hardly computer literate, but I know that if you delete files on a USB, you can sometimes retrieve them. Of course, I would not try to do this myself. There was one person who I thought could do this, and he was only fifteen minutes away.

When I got home, Rita was in bed. She said that she was feeling quite unwell again, and she'd been getting worse since the morning. I put a thermometer in her mouth. She was running a temperature and had not eaten and had only taken a few fluids. She tried to downplay it, but it was a concern. I called the clinic but only got a recorded message. It suggested taking two aspirin and if the problem persists calling the helpline. I decided I would call the MMC clinic in the morning and get their opinion. If things did not clear up, I would be visiting them in a hurry.

Once I had made sure that Rita was comfortable, I dropped in to see Arnold. When I told him what I required, he smiled and uttered the word "easy". Words I like to hear. He indicated that he would have a solution one way or the other in about twenty-five minutes.

I let him be, but Arnold was right. It only took him about twenty-five minutes. He was beaming when he knocked on my door. He had managed to extract several files that were of some interest. Of course, there was also a load of crap. I wasn't particularly interested in a list of Boston Pizzas or pharmacies that sold cut-price Viagra. There was also a list of clinics that would do hair transplants cheaply. I kept that one. I might use that later. But there were a couple of files that did interest me.

Corman had written to someone on the night before Connors' murder. We could not extract the entire file, but what we found was a letter written to someone called Larry. It said, "This should be straightforward. Send me more details and I'll make sure the job is carried out painlessly, at least for you. I understand that time is of the essence."

Very interesting, I thought but who the fuck was Larry? We might have been putting two and two together and making five, but this sounded like a contract for Connors' murder. Then again, perhaps, I was getting paranoid here. He could have been telling Larry that he was coming over to repair his toilet.

There was also a file with all the Uber drivers in North West Calgary listed. You may remember that the suicides had taken place in Uber vehicles. There was also a file on potassium chloride. I'd have to review this in more detail. God knows what that was all about. I had no idea what this stuff could be used for. It might have been used for snow removal, but perhaps Corman was worried about becoming potassium deficient.

I thanked Arnold for his help. I had detected the faint odour of marijuana in his house the day before. I would go over to the cannabis shop in the strip mall opposite that evening and get him a week's supply. I would have got some for myself, but Rita would have kicked my ass down the street. She just didn't like me using that stuff, at least not more than once a week. The pain of disobeying certainly wasn't worth the gain.

Before I prepared a Hungry Man dinner for Rita, I called Red and told him of the findings. He, too, was puzzled by the potassium chloride, though not completely. He didn't want to speculate, at least not yet. I also talked to Jen. I told her that this guy Bourne would be coming with me and that we should meet at the Rimrock Hotel for lunch before the conference. Now, I know what you are thinking if you know Banff. The Rimrock was way above my station, but Connors' had paid me a pisspot full of money and I only had three or four days to spend it. It was time to get the old mohair suit out again, but it was not all bad. Rita had bought me a silk tie for Christmas.

CHAPTER 13

I picked up Bourne from his apartment in Montgomery. In the old days, we would have thought of Bourne as a bit of a hippy. Long-haired and wearing John Lennon-type specs, he might have been one of those anorexic gits who did the full range of drugs years ago and worshipped at the feet of the Maharishi. His hair must have thinned considerably, and too much beer over the years had impacted his waistline a bit. He looked a bit like a Mr. 5 by 5 and walked with a pronounced limp. He'd been injured in a cross-country skiing accident years before.

I liked these sorts of characters. You could still imagine that he had the word 'peace' tattooed on his chest. He was a gentle soul, despite the slightly rough exterior. I gathered he was a very sensitive man. No need to say anymore. As we got into my truck, I realized I was partly correct. He had the letters 'peace' tattooed on his knuckles.

We took the back way to Banff down the 1A highway. This was so much more picturesque than the Trans-Canada Highway. It wasn't as quick and perhaps was a bit more dangerous, but I would go no other way. The road twisted and turned as it approached the mountains, which on this day were free of snow. There were some beautiful lakes, but many of them had frozen over. Despite this, you could almost imagine that it was spring, but this was the first week of January. The weather could turn nasty in a hurry and stay nasty for three or fourth months. I think Ted enjoyed the trip, though I'm sure that the Country and Western music that accompanied us was not exactly to his taste. We talked about MMC and the questionable past of some of the principals, but he wisely pointed out that these guys had friends in both high and low places and it would be wise to be careful. You would need a strong case to challenge them. They could end a career with one phone call. And a life, I mused to myself.

Banff usually was full of visitors with little or no parking, but things had changed over the last few months. Covid had done that. It was good now, albeit for the wrong reasons. Many of the businesses had suffered, and it was disappointing to witness the carnage, but it was a look at Banff, as it might have looked forty years ago.

We drove up to the Rimrock Hotel. This was probably the best situated hotel in Banff. It looked down on the town and even looked over the historic Banff Springs Hotel. We had arrived earlier than the others but decided to go into the dining room and await their entry. The staff were very accommodating. They even wondered if I would like to leave my baseball hat in the cloakroom. I think that was more of a suggestion than a request. I didn't want to lose that hat. I kept it with me.

We ordered a couple of beers and sat looking over the valley. You could see the Bow Falls in the distance behind the Banff Springs Hotel. It had been the scene of a Hollywood movie in the 1950s, starring Marilyn Monroe and Robert Mitchum. This was at a time when Banff was much less popular with tourists.

I asked Bourne about his career. He had always prided himself on being an investigative reporter, and he had a few major coups in Calgary. He described himself as a hard-hitting scribe who would always tease out the truth. At least that's what he said on his business card.

Moments later, Jen arrived with Chandra. I'd never met her before. She had been born in India but had lived most of her life in Western Canada. She had risen to the rank of department head in the Biomedical Department at the University but had since retired. Her focus had been on medical statistics and she had quite a reputation. She could always back up her opinions with data. Although she was only four foot eleven, apparently she could be a formidable foe. She was dressed in a green sari and was the picture of decorum and elegance. I began to regret not leaving my baseball cap in the cloakroom.

Although it might sound surprising, she and Bourne immediately found common ground and started nattering away. I focused more on baby talk with Jen. They had decided that their child would have an indigenous name. Albert or Tex were apparently out of the equation as, I suppose, was Sidney. No, it was going to be a traditional name. When it came to ordering food, I had no idea. I was up for sausages and mash, but that wasn't on the menu. Jen ordered something for me with a French name. Chandra and Bourne seemed to know what they wanted. Chandra had a snack. She told us she had eaten a plate of curried goat in mid-morning. All I could say was the food was fantastic, as was the service. Now I do have to say I like to see my plate full of food. There were bits here and there, decorating the plate like a work of art, but it tasted great, so I suppose it didn't matter. We were running a bit late, so I paid the bill and went overboard on the tip. Fifteen percent and worth every darn penny.

We drove down to the Banff Centre and made our way to the conference room. The meeting was entitled Biomedical Advances in the 21st Century and was being held in the Kinnear Centre. We had forgotten that attendance was by invitation only, but I knew how to bullshit our way in. I stood behind Chandra and told the officious guy at the desk that we were there from Mumbai and represented one of India's biggest hedge funds. I mean, do I look as if I come from Mumbai? The guy vacillated for a moment, but when she said that she had been invited by Bill Gates, he relented, and in we went. She was as good at bullshitting as I was.

The presentation by MMC was to come first. There were a few faces seated at the presentation table that I knew. There was Dr. Berryman, Lonnie Greene, and Sir Miles Garret. I'd seen their pictures in the newspaper the day before. They were also accompanied by two white-coated characters, a Dr. Steptoe and Dr. Prinsloo. I don't know whether they were proper doctors, but their major function appeared to be to look like doctors and nod wisely at the appropriate moments. They were described as the chief microbiologists on the project. In the rear was a white-coated, severe-looking woman named Dr. Susan Berryman. Obviously, Berryman's wife, except it wasn't. It was his sister.

This was a slick presentation, and they made Xyloleptokinase, sound as if it would revolutionize the medical profession. There were sporadic clappings and signs of approval that resonated throughout the hall. Call me a cynic, but I wondered if some of the audience were plants paid to show their approval. Then again, you could rely on most students to do that, anyway.

As the results were presented, I could see Chandra becoming more uncomfortable. I suppose it could have been the curried goat she'd eaten earlier in the day, but the way she was talking to Bourne, it was probably the results that were being presented. I guessed she found them discomforting. At the end of the presentation, there was a standing ovation, but then perhaps unwisely, from their perspective, they opened the floor to questions. There were a couple of slow lob questions and then Chandra started. Now, I couldn't tell you everything that she said. I didn't understand much of it. She said that the control group was inadequate and might lead to inappropriate conclusions. There was no proper placebo and there was no comment on any adverse effects, as there always are in drug trials. It seemed as if she was about to completely eviscerate the study. I could imagine that a few sphincters in that room were tightening.

It was inevitable that the chair would quickly call a halt to proceedings. He announced they had run out of time and any further questions could be addressed to the speakers after the meeting. He commented the MMC team was completely professional and could answer all the questions. As the speakers stepped down from the podium, they were surrounded by those sycophants who thought they gained credibility by mixing with the top dogs. If you looked at all threatening, there was a big lunk standing to the side. He looked as if he'd come from one of those French cave paintings. The sort of 'shall I hit him boss characters.' He had a badge on that said Dave. Why are all big lunks called Dave? I've yet to meet one called Mervyn.

Chandra was pissed, and she wasn't going to give up. She barged her way through the crowd. She had Bourne in tow. He was still copiously taking notes. They both had name badges on.

Chandra eventually cornered Berryman and Greene and announced that her colleague was Ted Bourne, the well-known columnist. They then used the age-old excuse that they were very busy and would welcome any questions about their research from anybody, even journalists. It seemed as if Mr. Bourne had a bit of a reputation. Greene said that if Mr. Bourne was going to write anything critical, he should submit it to the clinic for vetting. I thought this was complete bollocks. Greene pointed out that they had very good lawyers and a protracted legal fight would benefit nobody. I was standing a few feet away and almost added that it certainly wouldn't help their financing, but they were already on the way out of the room. Besides, Big Dave was beginning to look menacing. He'd pulled his shades down over his face and had gotten rid of his gum. There was one other thing. I thought I knew Big Dave, but how?

It was time for us to go and we drove down to Melissa's a pub/restaurant in the centre of Banff. The three of us shared a bottle of non-alcoholic wine. Jen had a Perrier water on the rocks. Again, the conversation was largely between Chandra and Ted. She carefully went through the flaws in the research and said that, in her view, this research should not be published. She then went on for about ten minutes about the inappropriate use of statistics. Of course, we didn't understand a word she was saying, but her passion made it clear that she knew what she was talking about. It was also clear that Ted thought he had a story and was going to get some mileage out of it. He said that the story would be out within the next few hours and certainly by the next day. This guy wasn't going to win the Pulitzer

Prize, but he realized he could make a bit of a name for himself. And then everyone calmed down. It sure wasn't the wine. It was probably a bit of fatigue. We decided to pop up to Mt. Norquay to watch the sun go down before we went home. Mt Norquay, a ski hill, overlooks the Banff town site. As the sun set and a myriad of colours emerged, I took out my flip phone and took a couple of pictures.

We all agreed that we would keep in touch and then we set off back to Calgary. It was a peaceful drive home. I had turned off the country and western. The journey was completed in relative silence. Little did we realize that this moment of peace and serenity would be the last we would have for some time. I shook hands with Bourne and suggested we should meet again very shortly.

When I got home, Rita was still ailing and at one point became a bit tearful. She didn't feel like eating. I tried to tempt her by ordering out from McDonald's. but that seemed to make her worse. Rita was a tough old bird, but I knew I would have to take her to the clinic the next morning. She simply wasn't doing very well. I told her to stop taking the experimental medication. It was simply not helping her very much. I wasn't going to make an appointment. We were just going to turn up and ask Berryman, or whoever was on duty, what the fuck was going on. I hoped we had not compromised Rita's situation with MMC because of our performance at the conference. I didn't trust those guys and I'm sure that they were not too fond of us. What this all had to do with Connors and her dead father, God only knew.

It was later that night that I received an e-mail from Bourne. He was good at his word. He sent me a copy of his article on MMC and it didn't pull any punches. This would not go down at all well. He was decent enough to provide MMC the chance to review the article, but he said that if they did not provide a rebuttal, it was likely to be published in less than twenty-four hours. Then he would be putting it on his website for all to see. Then the shit would hit the fan in a big way.

I sent the article to Red. He might still be up. There was a picture attachment, along with the article showing the speakers and the rest of the group as they left the auditorium. It was only about fifteen minutes later when Red called back. He was surprised by the article's candour, but even more amused by the photo. He'd immediately recognized the security guy and chuckled. This was big David Jessop, who used to fight with Pioneer Wrestling in the old days. Red had fought him a few times. I must have met him on a couple of occasions. While Dave was more renowned for his muscles than his brains, Red thought he might be a very useful contact in the future. He said that he would give Dave a call the next day. Red also noted that there had been no more threats to Jen, and she was beginning to feel more at ease. Perhaps it had just been a false alarm.

I was about to turn in for the night when Louie called. He was down at the casino. That was where he idled his free time playing poker. He said that he'd tried to get hold of me a couple of times during the day. Corman still had not been found, but there were reports he'd been seen on the opposite side of Nose Hill Park. He was driving the green truck. I didn't want to remind Louie that the cops were supposed to be surveilling this guy. They had dropped the ball on this one. What was it about Nose Hill Park that seemed to attract this guy? It couldn't have been the snowdrifts.

I did one final check on Rita. She was running a bit of a temperature. I thought of taking her to the Emergency Department but decided we would visit the experts at MMC in the morning, if, indeed, they were experts. I got Rita to bed and then did a bit of weed. I didn't want her to smell this stuff, so I stood on the porch and froze my arse off.

CHAPTER 14

It was obvious the Chinook couldn't last. There was a depression forming over Montana which inevitably would bring colder weather over Southern Alberta and possibly heavy snow. You never knew with Calgary being so close to the mountains. I remember years back; we had a heavy snow warning, and I cancelled all my appointments. It was sunny all day.

I was up first and started the truck outside to warm it up. Red had called earlier and said that he wouldn't mind accompanying Rita down to the clinic in the chance he might meet up with Dave Jessop. Red as usual arrived on time and as usual, I didn't have the coffee ready. Not exactly my fault. We'd been given one of those coffee machines that take cartridges, but all we had left was the candy cane flavour. I got out the instant stuff. You know the heavily caffeinated stuff that would tighten your socks just by sniffing it.

We all squeezed into the truck. Rita had not improved, and her breathing was not good. Minutes later, we were escorting her into the elevator, which led up to the clinic. When we walked in the receptionist demanded to know whether we had an appointment or not. We told her we didn't need one. Rita was ill and needed help. She was about to turn us away when I told her I would call the press about this if we didn't get some satisfaction. She began to answer and then I became aware that she was looking over my shoulder. If there was ever a look of apprehension, this was it. I turned. Berryman was standing there. He looked like shit. It probably had something to do with Bourne's article. He must have read it by now. Then again, he could have been banging the receptionist all night. I opted for the former.

"How can I help you, Mr........,?" he said.

"Arbuckle," I replied assertively. "Sidney Arbuckle." At least, he hadn't called me Rita's intended. "And you can help her out right now. She's on your drug trial and is feeling like shite." At least, I'd kept my true feelings in check.

"Well, we'll do some tests and see what we can find out. I'm sure we can help the little lady."

The patronizing bastard. If Rita had been feeling well, I'm sure she would have told him to go and suck the big one. But she smiled weakly. Perhaps she'd been impressed with the little lady reference.

"Yeah, well make it quick," said Red. "I don't want to see my mother suffer." That was quite clever. I mean, he had to have a valid reason for being there, not that he looked anything like his supposed 'mother'. He dwarfed her by about sixteen inches.

Berryman called for a nurse, but she did not immediately appear.

"These sorts of things are quite rare and nothing to worry about. Just a few blood tests, possibly an x-ray, and we'll see what the problem is. She'll be just fine." He was starting to pace, which, in my view suggested anxiety. How the fuck could he know that she'd be fine? I wasn't about to argue.

The nurse eventually appeared. Berryman looked at his watch and made it obvious that he was doing so. She was in for a bollocking behind the scenes. They disappeared with Rita into the inner sanctum of the clinic.

We sat there in silence until a few minutes later big Dave Jessop walked in. Now let me tell you a bit about Dave. Red had filled me in on the way over. Dave Jessop was not his wrestling name. Let's face it, the name Dave Jessop doesn't sell too many tickets in professional wrestling. He went by the name of Ivan Borlzoff, the Chernobyl terror. He would come into the ring draped in the Russian flag and sing the Russian National Anthem. There was just one problem, the nearest Dave had been to Russia was when he drove a truck to Swift Current. And he couldn't speak a word of Russian. He just mumbled the anthem. He also had this shtick with women. After a bout, he would go up to them and say "Heh, I'm hot baby and I'm just about to go critical." It never worked. As Red said, he was the only wrestler he ever knew who'd never got laid after a show. He used to have body odour, which didn't help. Anyway, most of the fans probably thought Chernobyl was a rock group and just wouldn't get the joke.

Time hadn't been good to Dave. The only use for the world championship belt would have been for Dave to hold his gut in. But he immediately recognized Red.

"Red, you dickhead. No long. No time see." Now, I realized he'd fucked that up, but this was a really friendly welcome. You see, that's how guys greet each other.

"Davie, you colossal piece of horseshit, it's great to see you."

You could feel the bonding experience beginning to develop.

Red introduced me to Dave. He said I was a good friend who had brought his wife in for an assessment. We spoke too loudly. The receptionist must have been listening.

'If you're her son, she said to Red, then that guy must be your father. She pointed at me. "You don't look a bit like your son. He looks...he looks..."

"Go on, say it," I said.

"Indian."

"He is," I said. Born in Delhi. I told him to leave his turban at home."

"So how can you be his father?" she said.

"Stepfather," I said. "Stepfather. And we still are good friends."

"Oh, I see," she said. Of course, she didn't see because that would have meant Rita was born in Delhi.

Red and Dave then indulged in a bit more banter before deciding the conversation was getting a bit too adult. They excused themselves and went outside into the corridor. While this was going on, one of the clinic nurses came out and said they would be doing some exploratory X-rays. Nothing to worry about, which usually is the time you start worrying.

After about ten minutes, Red reappeared. He said that Dave was just going off duty but would meet us half an hour later at the pub across the road. He wasn't employed by the clinic but was employed by a Security Company to provide a bit of muscle if it was needed. It would be interesting to talk to him. I wondered if he had easy access to the clinic after hours.

It seemed like an eternity, probably because I was worrying so much, but Rita appeared about 30 minutes later with Dr. Steptoe. Remember, we had seen him at the conference the day before. He indicated that she still had a small blood clot and that they were taking her off the trial. She would be placed back on another drug, Warfarin. This was the rat poison drug I'd previously mentioned. I suppose they had to use it for something. Alberta was officially rat-free. I'd already done my research. He thanked us for our participation and said that he was grateful that Rita had signed the non-disclosure agreement which required us to keep our mouths shut. We could keep the options that were part of the agreement if we did. Look, the non-disclosure agreement was a big pisser to me, but I wasn't going to say anything in there. We could talk about it later. As we left, we passed Dave out in the corridor.

"It was nice to meet you, Sidney," he said. People are funny, aren't they? I hadn't even said a word to him except 'hello.'

I think it was the news that she was not in any imminent danger that perked Rita up. She was certainly in the mood for a glass of wine, but we decided we would do this at home. We would let Red meet with Dave in the pub. Red was a sharp guy and if there was information to get from Dave, Red would certainly get it.

When we got home, I made sure Rita was comfortable and then decided to see if I could get hold of Bourne. I hoped he had not been warned off. Despite several calls, we could not get him. I emailed him and told him to get hold of me pronto. I even called the local newspaper, but because he was a freelance journalist, they couldn't help me find him, at least not immediately. I just hoped he would get back to me.

When Red got back to our place, it was obvious that he'd had a few glasses of wine. Now Red was essentially a non-drinker, but if it was in the call of duty, he would consider it. He said that Dave was not a favourite of the MMC clinic and was not afraid to answer questions. Dave described Berryman as an elephant's dongle. That was the word the lads in the business used to call someone a big prick. Not surprisingly, he found Berryman to be full of himself, arrogant and conceited. Not sure he would have used those exact words, but I certainly got the gist. He also said that there were a few oddities about the clinic. Red had done an amazing job. He said that Dave had let him borrow his pass card, but he would have to get it back by the afternoon. I wondered if we could copy it. He had already given Red the password to gain entry. If we went in there overnight, I'm not sure what we hoped to find, but something was going on. I wanted to see what Mrs. Connors' involvement was.

Now, under normal circumstances, I suspect that copying the card would have been impossible, but we didn't have a normal circumstance living next door to us. I told Red to leave it with me and I would see what I could do. I immediately walked next door and rang Arnold's doorbell. He had set it up so the lights would flash on and off when there was someone at the door. No answer. Course, that happened the first time I tried to get him. I rushed back to my computer and e-mailed him. "Open the fuckin door", I said. He replied, "I've got a fucking woman in here, bugger off." Two minutes later, he was at my door. He was either a very quick worker, had erectile problems, or was taking the piss. I assumed the latter. He did utter something which sounded like "taking the piss" but it was not very clear.

I carefully asked Arnold whether he could copy the security card. He typed out that it would be difficult, but certainly not impossible.

He would give it a try. But he did warn me he actually had a girlfriend coming over later that afternoon. I told him he should bring her over for drinks that night. He nodded and then disappeared.

To be honest, I never really considered that Arnold had a girlfriend. I couldn't have been more wrong. Red and Jen would have hammered me for negative profiling or something. They say that some women go for the strong, silent types and others say that women often go for somebody with a brain. That's why I was not particularly successful with women. I wasn't silent and could never convince them I was endowed with a brain, though I always made it clear that I had very big feet. Arnold definitely passed the test on both scores, though I'd never looked at his feet.

About an hour later, a rather nice car drove up. I think it was a Jaguar. Not the sort of car you'd want to leave in our neighbourhood overnight. And a classy, if somewhat mature bird emerged. Now I'm no expert on class. To be honest, if you have your own teeth, don't wear a tracksuit, and don't have an AC-DC tattoo on your cheek, you qualify, but this lady seemed to be in the next echelon. She disappeared into the house. She had her own key. Holy shit, I was tempted to e-mail Arnold and warn him that this could be a slippery slope. Women can get in the way, especially if you're trying to copy a password.

I doubted Arnold could pull this off, but about two hours later there he was at the door with a pass card plus the original one in an envelope. I mean there was no assurance that this copy would work. And he'd worked out the password.

I hadn't asked Rita about this, but I thought it would be nice if I asked Arnold and his lady friend over for drinks and a few snacks later that evening. Rita was feeling better. We could always order in from the new venture in town called 'Skip the Frying Pan.' Arnold agreed and, thank goodness, Rita was quite intrigued by the idea. I told him to get there after seven and to make sure he brought his girlfriend. Then I had a bad thought. What if she wasn't a girlfriend? You know what I mean.

I immediately phoned Red and called him to come on over. We only had about half an hour to get the pass card to Jessop. We should also ask him what the best time would be to enter the premises. It would probably have to be in the middle of the night, but best to check with Dave. Red arrived, and we agreed on a plan. He suggested we should get Jessop to test the new card. No point in arriving at 3.00 AM with a card that didn't work. Red called Jessop and he agreed to do it. Red slipped away for about thirty minutes to get the pass card back to Dave and to make sure the copy worked. Dave took his pass card back and confirmed that the pass was for the back entrance of the building., There was a nurse on duty in the reception area most of the night. He thought that the best time to go in would be about 3:00 a.m.

Because Red would be away for much of the night, we decided it might be appropriate for Jen to stay over at our place for the night. There would be another two guests for dinner. Thank goodness that Connors had paid us such a nice retainer.

It all worked out as planned. Everybody arrived on schedule. Arnold and his partner arrived first. It transpired that his girlfriend was also partially deaf, but she could understand us quite well. When Arnold introduced her, he pointed at her and said.

"This is Dephne"

I think he was trying to say Daphne, but it came out wrong. Sounded like deaf knee. I nearly pissed myself laughing but good manners and the fact that Rita had grabbed me by the balls saved the situation.

Daphne smiled and said that Arnold would have to practice saying her name. It sometimes came out wrong. She then introduced herself as Daphne. A difficult moment passed. They were certainly very attentive to each other. I could see that Rita was very impressed by this. Later in the evening, Rita asked me why we couldn't be much more like that. "What?" I replied as I held my hand to my ear. "You say something?" She was not at all impressed.

Having six for dinner sort of messed things up, and I suggested we should order some fish and chips. I was not sure they all would appreciate fish and chips, but I was wrong. Daphne was even more enthusiastic. She had been born in Manchester, just a few miles away from where I was born. When she was a kid, she said that she used to eat fish and chips out of newspapers, but they banned it because of the lead in the newsprint. She was disappointed that there weren't mushy peas with it. Mushy peas still seemed to be a bit of a delicacy in parts of England. Anyway, I knew she was from the U.K. Her signing was done with an obvious English accent.

The boxes of fish and chips disappeared quickly until there was only one piece of fish left.

"Anybody want the last piece of fish?" said Rita. Now we've all been in this sort of situation before. Everybody looks at everybody else uncomfortably. I'm of the opinion that if you want it, then own up. After ten seconds, I said that I might as well have it and grabbed it. Rita told me later that doing that was ungracious. But I know how this works. Nobody takes it and after three or four days in the fridge, it gets thrown out.

After supper, Rita suggested we should all watch a movie. Now I thought that this was a bit of a problem because of Daphne's and Arnold's hearing problems. Daphne suggested we watch a film with subtitles. Now I must admit if it doesn't have sex, drugs, rock and roll, and a bit of action, then it's not for me. But Red and Jen were up for it, so what could I say? We watched an Iranian film. No idea what it was called. About some kid who lost his sneakers. Didn't sound much to me, but I gritted my teeth and hoped I wouldn't fall asleep. Well, surprise, surprise. What a brilliant movie! I won't be giving up on Sex Maidens of the Galaxy, but I'd be up for watching the Iranian version with subtitles.

It had been a really successful evening. I think we all enjoyed it. It was nice to meet Daphne. She seemed to have a bit of class. I wondered if some might rub off on me. And I was able to find out about her apparent affluence. Her husband had died, and he had a rather sizable life insurance policy against his name. I thought Arnold was onto a good thing here. Why had this never happened to me?

That was just the start of the evening for Red and me. We had the pass card and decided to visit the clinic at about three in the morning. Since the clinical trial was over, there would be no patients in the clinic and, hopefully, nobody else, or so we hoped. If the trial was over, it was unlikely that a nurse would be on duty, but we would still go in through the rear entrance. Jessop had told us that there were security inspections at 2 and 4 in the morning. That would give us plenty of time to explore. We were not sure what we were looking for, but there might be some interesting documentation to be found.

It was minus 35 degrees C when we reached the clinic. It was adjacent to a shopping mall, and we decided it might be better to park away from the clinic. No point in making it obvious by parking outside the building. There were probably security cameras.

We sidled, as unobtrusively as possible, towards the clinic, but there couldn't have been anyone within miles. We made sure our identities were hidden by our hoods and face scarves. There was not much choice. It was that cold. Getting into the clinic was not difficult. The elevators were not working, but we used the emergency stairs. I was glad that Red had brought a flashlight, otherwise, we would have been screwed. We used the pass card to get in through the rear entrance. No alarm sounded. We went first to the clinic office, where we thought all the records would be kept. There was nothing that was easily accessible, but we hit the jackpot when we went into what we assumed to be Berryman's office. He had left his computer on and we were able to download some files that were showing on the screen. There seemed to be a list of patients, their progress notes, and eventual outcomes. I took out a USB and copied the files. We also copied some paper files on the photocopier. And then there was what might have been a password taped to the desk. It was either for his computer or his cell phone or perhaps it was a password for a pornographic site. We would have to find out.

Before I go any further, I knew we were breaking the law and it would be career-ending if we were caught. In fact, things could not have gone better, but it changed suddenly when all the main lights in the clinic went on. We heard a security guard talking on his radio. He said that he was going to do a quick check of the building. Fuck Jessop. He'd been completely wrong. I suspect he would have been confused by a three-count in wrestling.

It looked as if we were trapped. There did not appear to be an alternative way out, but there was a door to the side of Berryman's office. We went through it. It was barely lit with blue light, but we could tell right away that it was a small operating room. I mean you could tell by the smell of antiseptics. We looked for somewhere to hide. There was a small cupboard to the side which Red got into. Good for him, but I was trapped, or was I?

I spotted a white sheet and picked it up. I lay on the operating table and covered myself from head to toe with the sheet. I heard the security guard walk into the theatre. I was aware that he was surveilling the room with a flashlight. I tried not to breathe. My wheezing, caused by too many cigs, would give me away. It was just as he was leaving that the events of the night caught up with me. I've always had a bit of a dodgy tummy, but I had eaten too much of the fish and chips. I mean, I knew it was coming. You always do. Could I hang on long enough? I couldn't. Just as he closed the door, I farted rather loudly. When he opened the door seconds later, I thought I was done. Now I couldn't see him, but Red could. Apparently, he looked around for a few seconds, sniffed, and then closed the door. Perhaps he was deaf. But I wasn't I could hear him reporting back to base. He said that he thought there was a problem with the air filtration system in the operating room, and they should check it out in the morning. Who the fuck did he think was on the operating table? A dead body. Thank god there was someone else out there with Dave Jessop's brains.

After that, we decided to wait for about ten minutes before leaving the building. I hoped it had been a successful night. I noticed Louie had called me several times. It seemed as if it was urgent. I wasn't going to call him in the middle of the night, though he probably would have answered. I dropped off Red at his house and slipped into bed a few minutes later. Rita was snoring, but I tucked myself up beside her. I was frozen.

In the couple of minutes, before I fell asleep, I began to think over some of the events of the past, especially as they related to Connors' murder. And then I had what I hoped was a eureka moment. I thought back to the telephone logs, which showed that there had been two calls from the clinic to Connors the night before her murder. I'd always assumed that I had made both of them. When I thought about it carefully, I realized I had made only one call from the clinic's phone. I had made the other from my cell phone. The question was who from the clinic had made the other phone call and why. Within moments, I must have fallen asleep. I just hoped I would remember this eureka moment in the morning. I usually didn't.

CHAPTER 15

The following morning, Rita decided to let me sleep in. I was exhausted and didn't reach a decent level of consciousness until about ten 'o'clock. I lay in bed for a few minutes. I hadn't forgotten my eureka moment from the night before. In fact, I remembered it more clearly.

When I used the clinic phone, I remembered that Berryman had been standing behind me. He obviously remembered what I had said to Connors. I would have to check our notes. Did I make the first call and Berryman the second? I had only made one call on their lines. As I was thinking about this Rita appeared with a cup of coffee. That was very nice of her. She'd usually kick me out of bed, and I'd make the coffee. She also told me that Louie had called. She thought it was very urgent. He had said to her, "Rita get dumb fuck out of bed" He didn't usually swear with Rita, at least not like that.

I got up and immediately dialled Louie. I don't know whether you have ever done this, but I was taking a piss when I got through to him. The dialogue went something like this.

"Hi Lou, what's happening?"

"Heh, you taking piss."

'Well,.....er......er...as a matter of fact I am."

"You sit down. You'll shit yourself when you hear this."

"What is it?" I said.

"Corman's been found dead."

"I'm sitting down Lou. Tell me more."

"Early this mornink. Body found near 14th Street Bridge. He must have jumped. Landed on ice. Just removing body in a few minutes. You get here. Out. "

I was off the shitter in a second. I was in shock. I didn't need this. Our only suspect was dead. I downed my coffee, kissed Rita goodbye, put on my winter coat, and jumped in the truck. I hadn't realized until now the heater didn't work very well. Not a problem. I was a prairie boy now. I could put up with this. And I didn't have any windscreen washer to melt the ice. Not a problem. I had a bottle of hand sanitizer. Don't suppose you know this, but it works just as well.

I got down to 14th Street as fast as I could. The police had cordoned off the area though the body had been moved by the time I got there. Louie waved me through the cordon. He said that the body had been found early in the morning by a passerby. It looked as if the deceased had either jumped or been thrown over the bridge and landed on a sheet of ice. The river was beginning to freeze over. A few more days at these temperatures and it would be completely frozen over. I asked whether the body had been identified. It had. C.orman had a daughter who had been contacted. She identified the body right away. The body had Corman's wallet on it with all his ID and his green truck had been found just across the bridge. But I wanted to be sure. Just my paranoid nature.

"Look, Louie. Did the body have any other identifying features?" I said.

"Nothing really. He did have a few track marks on his arm."

"A druggy?" I asked.

"Perhaps, but probably nothing serious."

"Anything else?"

"Looked as he had a puncture mark on his arm and his fist was grasping a tuft of hair that wasn't his."

"So, you're thinking it was murder?" I said.

"Who's to say? It did look as if he got a big blow to the back of his head, but he could have got that in the fall."

"If it was murder," I said. "Any suspects?"

"Guys like Corman have more enemies than I have hot dinners. But if he was murdered, we'll find them for sure," he said. I liked his confidence.

"What now?"

"They'll get the body autopsied. Once we've found out the cause of death, we can take the next step forward. We know by the morning."

I thanked Louie. There was nothing much to see. Besides, I was freezing my ass off standing outside. I told him that I would keep in touch with him and then I jumped in the truck and made my way home. On the way back, I thought I might as well call Bourne. I hadn't talked to him in a while and I was beginning to worry. I dropped into the nearest Tims and dialled his number. I just hoped that he had not been persuaded to drop the story. I'd seen that happen before. Still no reply. Perhaps he'd taken the big pay-off. This entire investigation was getting fucked up. In a way, it was over for us. We had found out what had happened to Connors' father, and we'd even discovered who bumped her off. But it was all a bit too easy. We still didn't clearly understand the motivation behind it all. I called Red and suggested we go over the case after lunch.

When I got home, I looked at the documents we had received the morning before. I thought that the USB might hold a trove of information. It listed all the clinic files, but when I tried to open any of them, I discovered they were password-protected. I wondered if Arnold might help us yet again, but he and Daphne had arranged to go up to the Kananaskis for the day to take in the scenery and take some photographs. It seemed that they both had a passion for photography, and they would certainly get some amazing shots in that area.

I must admit that Arnold was showing us a great sense of humour. When I asked him later what he liked about Kananaskis, he took his keyboard and typed out "I love the silence" He smiled for a few moments.

Red arrived shortly after lunch. I half expected Jen to be with him, but she had managed to get in touch with Bourne. He had left a text message on her phone. She had arranged to meet him later that day if he was available. It was all mysterious. Why the fuck wouldn't he answer my calls? Perhaps I lacked charm.

Red had told Jen to stay in touch. He was still a bit worried about her.

When Red arrived, we examined some of the files we had xeroxed. Most of them referred to clinical progress notes, and it was difficult to work out who was who. The names were coded so you would have to have the key to decipher them. Hopefully, this was somewhere else on the USB. It was password-protected, and we'd have to find a way to break it.

One thing we did notice was that there had been quite a few dropouts from the trial. Out of 105 participants, nine had dropped out. This was signified by the word deleted against each code number. We would have to do our best to find out who these people were and why they were excluded.

I had also found a file on the USB. It said Berryman CHPG. We had come across that abbreviation before on the prescription label. If only we could open that file. There was also a file labelled Connors. What the fuck was that all about? We decided that there was not a lot more we could do until we could access the USB drive. Red called Jen and suggested that she meet him at my place after she had met Bourne. That should have been a couple of hours ago.

It was only then that I realized that I still had the password that I had found on Berryman's desk. It was comprised of numbers. I tried using it to open up the USB computer files, but people don't, in my limited experience, use numbers for a password. It didn't work. And then Red had a brilliant idea. Perhaps the numbers were the passcode for Berryman's cell phone. There was only one way to find out. But first, we would have to find out what his cell phone number was. I decided that either Red or Jen could look after that. Which rather begged the question. Where was Jen? It wasn't like her not getting back to us.

Moments later, we saw Arnold arrive back from his sojourn in the country. He did it in style. He slowly climbed out of the Jaguar carrying what appeared to be a very expensive camera. Just for the show. What's wrong with using your cell phone? Well, not my cell phone. I still didn't know how to use the camera.

As Daphne drove away, I waved for Arnold to come in. He wasn't in a talkative mood, but then he never was. I asked him if it was at all possible to read the files without the appropriate password. He shook his head but then typed out, 'But I know somebody who could.' He then put his finger to his lips as if to say, 'But shut the fuck up.' We gave him the USB and sent him on his way. If this took another Iranian film about a kid with sneakers, it would be all worth it. Alright, I'll tell you a secret. I would have willingly watched another Iranian film. The first one was that good.

While Red was waiting for Jen to arrive, I looked at my e-mails. There was a brief note from Louie. He said that the initial indications about Corman suggested a blunt force trauma possibly caused by the fall from the bridge. It showed that this was likely a result of a suicide. Not another one and, in my view, not believable in such a hard-core crook. Then there was bad news. The official cause of death was suicide exacerbated by the chronic effects of Covid. As I read this out, Red burst out laughing. "What the fuck?" he said. Now, this was unusual for Red, since you rarely heard him swear. I knew why he was upset. His uncle on the reservation had a massive heart attack about three months previously. He died before they could get him to the hospital. He was diagnosed as dying from Covid. Red thought it was all a scam. He would not be taking the vaccine this year or any year.

I realized that the investigation was not complete, but the idea of a killer such as Corman committing suicide seemed absurd to me. The anti-social narcissist never commits suicide. Perhaps, he had sneezed, concluded that he had Covid, and offed himself because he was a threat to humanity. Complete bollocks. Criminals are quite egocentric and don't give a fuck about anybody else. I just hoped that further investigation would provide more light on the situation.

There was very little in my mailbox except for a promotional message from the Calgary Pro Arte Theatre Group. They were putting on a new show. It was a streamed version of a new thriller called Suicide by Cyanide. Crappy title. Did we want tickets? The previous one was O.K, I suppose, but I shook my head.

"What's that all about?" said Red.

"Remember the Calgary Pro-Arte Theatre Group. You bought us tickets. Remember, it was a murder mystery."

"I do. What was it like?" said Red. "Worth the few hundred dollars we paid for the tickets?"

"That's bullshit," I replied. "Jen told me they were complimentary."

"Complimentary to you," he said and laughed. "Did you solve the mystery?"

"Well, it was very muddled....too complicated. A bit like this case."

"I'll ask you again," he said. "Did you solve the mystery, Sid?"

"It was the sort of case that needed a good private eye to solve it. If somebody in the public had got it right, it could only have been dumb luck. So, we, the experts, inevitably solved it."

"Jen told me it was Arnold who solved it." Red laughed.

"Bullshit. He got an assist," I said.

"All right, what exactly does the invite say?"

"The CPTG wants to invite you to our streamed production of Suicide by Cyanide on January 10th."

"Just a minute. What did you say?"

"Suicide by Cyanide."

"No, who was putting it on? Just give me the letters."

"CPTG. Holy shit! I see what you mean. Those were the initials that we saw on the pill bottles. Remember, we thought it was......it was."

"A pharmacy," I replied. "We're going to have to put the pieces together and see how it all fits. Why the fuck would Sykes have a pill bottle on him that said CPTG?"

"I think we'll have time for that in due course," said Red. "But now, I'm really worried about Jen. It just isn't like her to stay out of touch. After that threat, I might be getting paranoid, but you can't take any chances. I haven't spoken to her all day. I mean, it's a bit early to put out a missing person's report."

"Where was she meeting Bourne?" I said.

"That's the problem, she didn't say. Look, I'm going to go home right now and see if she's there."

As he was leaving, his cell phone rang. It was Jen. Some of the colour re-emerged in his face. I made an excuse to leave the room. You didn't want to be part of that sort of conversation between a man and a wife. When I got back three minutes later, Red was positively vibrant. It didn't seem to matter that Bourne had not turned up. Jen was safe. Her cell phone battery had died, and she had no way of charging it. She'd had problems with that battery. It wasn't charging very well. So, with a couple of hours to spare, she decided to buy a new pair of shoes. Now, we men understand full well that a woman doesn't just spend two hours looking for a new pair of shoes. Alright, Rita spends a lot less time but there's not much of a choice in sneakers at Pay Value shoes. And I think I've wasted precious time if I take two minutes to buy a pair of shoes. I'm serious. Did I mention that Jen never actually bought a pair after several hours of shopping?

All was forgiven. The crisis was over on one front. But there was a crisis on another front. Where the fuck was Bourne?. He must have gotten cold feet, but Jen was not one to avoid a difficult situation. She had read Bourne's piece and was unlikely to let it lay fallow. Her position was that if Bourne would not publish on his website, she would tackle Berryman about it as soon as she could. She said she would send a missive off overnight and she would make sure it got on the internet and that Berryman would know it.

Red left to get together with his wife and I went into the kitchen to prepare a haute cuisine meal. It was to be freeze-dried curried beef without the frills. I bet Chandra wouldn't turn her nose up at that, though Rita might.

I had just gotten the rice in the microwave when my cell phone rang. It was Louie. He had some news. They had searched Corman's truck. They found an unsigned suicide note. It was the typical 'I can't go on' shite. At least there wasn't a pill bottle to go with it. He also told me that there had been a few drops of blood found on the front seat of the truck. The police were going to check to see if it was Corman's, though how they were going to do this in a hurry I couldn't imagine. Louie was no fool. He realized that this was altogether too bizarre. He finished up with his typical Romanian salvo. "Smell like horseshit,", he said.

Surprisingly, Rita enjoyed the beef curry. These things were on sale. I'd go down to the store the next day and buy a stack of them. You had a choice. There was curried chicken, prawns, and pork. I decided against the curried sausage, though admittedly that was 75% off.

We sat down for a bit of relaxation that night. The Best of Dancing with Stars was on for two hours followed by 'Cook Off'. I might start saying "cook off" instead of.....You get the idea. Much more civilized.

Before I sat down for a night of boredom, I checked out our stock. It was still doing very well. I almost thought of calling Jen and asking her to back off in her criticisms but thought better of it. It might affect the stock price.

I somehow survived the TV bonanza and was just getting into my pajamas when there was a tap on the front door. It was Arnold. He was looking very pleased with himself. He uttered something indecipherable, but I guessed he had been successful in breaking the password. I invited him in. He told me via his tablet that a colleague had worked out the password, but it would be at a cost. That was a bugger, but It was only two hundred bucks. We could live with that. He wanted to get going there and then. Much as I wanted to take him up on the offer,

I had to decline. It was just too late, and I was knackered. It could wait until the morning. Remember, I was quite sleep-deprived. God knows how I stayed awake during Dancing with the Stars. I told him we'd start nice and early......at about 10.45 AM. I had to say goodnight. The curried prawns were beginning to have a one-way dialogue with me.

Before he left, I asked him if the password number we had found could be for a phone messaging system. He thought that it could. That, too, could be looked at tomorrow.

CHAPTER 16

Perhaps something had been lost in the translation. Arnold arrived at 8:45 a.m. Much too early for me and probably much too early for Arnold. I was already up, and I noticed Daphne's car outside his house. I thought he'd be late this morning for sure. It would be nookie time if I was him. Been there, worn the 't-shirt, albeit quite a few years back. I was wrong. There he was, ready to begin work.

I wasn't ready for much of anything. I looked a mess. I was still in my underwear. I hadn't shaven and hadn't put my plate in and just hadn't any time for my fibre supplement. I wasn't going to turn him away. He'd just have to put up with me at the breakfast table. I soon learned what the two hundred dollars was for. Photocopying. He was carrying a box of papers about a foot thick. It was going to take an age to go through all of this. Most of it was probably useless, at least to us. Pages upon pages of laboratory results. Serial creatine tests would not help us, and I really didn't need to know that one patient had an undescended testicle. And we'd have to destroy much of this stuff. Confidential medical information and all that.

I offered Arnold a candy cane coffee, and he accepted. I then contacted Red. It looked like we were going to have a busy day.

As we sat in front of the TV news, sipping coffee, the business portion came on. Now I must admit I've been naïve about how to use our new TV. You could get the news with captions underneath for the deaf. That was helpful to Arnold, though he didn't seem that interested. As I sat there sipping my coffee, I wondered. Could we get Sex Maidens of the Galaxy, with captions though to be fair there wasn't much dialogue in that movie. Anyway, any dialogue wouldn't affect the plot. Now I hope you realize I am joshing with you. My sex drive used to be on Automatic, but it has been stuck in Park for a few years now.

We were going to have the place to ourselves that morning. Rita volunteered at the Food Bank for much of the day. As she left, I saw she was carrying the case of freeze-dried curries out to her car. Now if she thought they were such crap, why inflict them on the hungry? No, she must have thought they were brilliant, and she was doing society a favour.

When Red arrived, he had some very interesting news. Jen had been involved in a bit of a bust-up with Berryman and she told him in no uncertain terms that she was going to publish an article about her misgivings about the research. To say that he was upset was a bit of an understatement. Berryman had slammed the phone down. Nice work Jen. I would have done anything to knock that prick off his perch.

Things were about to get even better. Bourne was back on side. He sent her a text message to her apologizing for his lack of balls and agreed to meet her at the North Hill Shopping Centre just opposite the LRT station. Plenty of parking there, especially since all the Covid restrictions. They were supposed to meet at two that afternoon. Red had already talked to Louie, who agreed to send a copy of Corman's suicide note over. Red was darn good. You could rely on him at all times, which was why, in a few years, I had him slated to take over from me as president of Lou Diamond Investigations.

We had just started our conversation when Daphne appeared. I quickly put on my trousers. I didn't know this, but she had arranged with Rita to help at the Food Bank. I mentioned Rita had already gone. It was just around the corner. She was a real find, this one. She explained that even deaf people needed food. If Arnold let Daphne slip away, I'd give him a kick in the arse so hard he wouldn't be silent anymore.

Once the girls had gone, we got down to business, minus Arnold. He mentioned he had other business to attend to that morning. Probably going off to rewrite Einstein's theory of relativity.

We thought that the thing that might bring immediate results was Berryman's phone. Could we gain access using the numbers we'd found on his desk? We waited, with bated breath, as we dialled his number. Thank god he didn't answer, but his receptionist did. "Dr. Berryman is indisposed and not taking messages," she said. Probably still in a funk after Jen's conversation with him a few hours before.

I tried to access his inbox and when it asked for the password number, I carefully dialled in the numbers we had found. Bingo. I was in. There were 65 messages that I could access. This was going to take an age. I went back to the very first messages, which went back to the time of Connors' murder. There was some interesting stuff there. It seemed as if Berryman was having an affair with someone and I'm not making this up, called Modesty. Red said he had probably ordered her from 'Skip the Vows.' Darn it. Rita never talked to me the way Modesty talked to Berryman

.

We quickly turned that message off. It was simply getting just too explicit. And then we hit the jackpot. There were two messages of interest. One came from Mrs. Connors. She told Berryman to call her urgently. She knew what had happened to her father, and she needed an explanation. This was just after we had left the clinic for the first time. The second message was even more relevant. Corman had called Berryman late that night to tell him he could look after things at a price and that he thought Berryman would pay. We skipped to the more recent messages. There was one from Lonnie Greene. He said that he had heard about this Bourne character. Adverse publicity could blow the whole fucking thing out of the water, according to Greene. He also wondered where the fuck Corman was. He asked Berryman to get back to him urgently. That was early yesterday.

The most recent message was a muffled one from Corman stating that the cops were after him and he'd had enough. There's only one way out. You'll read about me in the papers. It would have been useful if we could have gotten Berryman's responses to these messages, but we certainly had enough to chew over for the time being. At the very least, it provided some support for my eureka moment. It looked as if the second call from the clinic had not been me after all but from Berryman. I wondered if Connors was trying to blackmail Berryman. I suppose it was possible. It also added a lot more. It showed a strong link between Berryman, Greene, and Corman. That information would have been particularly damaging for Berryman and Greene and the project, for that matter.

I looked at Red for his opinion. He agreed with me. The big issue was what we were going to do with this information. We could contact the police, but except for Louie, it didn't really make sense. I knew they would be uninterested and now Corman was dead, they'd be even less interested. They could sew this case up nicely, thank you very much and they could resume looking for speeders on Deerfoot Trail the same day.

Red thought we would have to take the initiative and, by this, he suggested visiting Berryman right away. That was a good idea. At the conference, it was mentioned that Dr. Berryman would be flying to New York on Friday. That was tomorrow. If he was still in town, we needed to ask him a few questions. No point in calling him and asking him for an appointment. He would make some excuse and we wouldn't see him for a while, if ever. We decided we would go over to the clinic right away. After that, we could hopefully spend the afternoon going through the rest of the purloined USB files.

We were at the clinic twenty minutes later. When we arrived at the receptionist's desk, we were told that Dr. Berryman was in conference. We told him it was extremely important that he unconference himself. It was extremely urgent. Moments later, he emerged.

"Two gentlemen to see you, Larry," she said. Holy shit, this was Larry. Dr. Lawrence Berryman. We'd missed that. Lawrence equalled Larry. I admit we could be dumb at times.

He invited us into his office and sat down. Although he looked his usual arrogant self, you could tell that he was uneasy. Now one thing that you must recognize is that we couldn't be too truthful. This meant we could not reveal that we had tapped his phone.

"What can I do for you gentlemen?" he said.

"We have received some reports that there are some doubts about the research project," I said.

"I can assure you, we have no concerns about it. There are always doubters out there. In fact, we welcome healthy criticism. It's easily handled." With that, he picked up the newspaper on his desk and pointed with his finger at an article at the bottom of the financial page. It said.

'Conspiracy theorists question the new MMC study. Journalist Ted Bourne, who was once described as a member of the flat earth society...'

I didn't finish the article though Red did. This was the same old shit that they would wheel out when you disagreed with convention and certainly when you disagreed with a pharmaceutical company. They probably had him believing in lizard people and fake moon landings.

"Ad hominem attacks prove nothing," said Red. "This doesn't answer the criticisms of your study." Now I had no fucking idea what an ad hominem attack was. I hoped they weren't having a go at Bourne's sexuality. That could get you into trouble these days.

"Nobody ever believes that rubbish," said Berryman. "Someone inventing a story. The science is settled."

"That's the most unscientific statement I have ever heard," replied Red. "But I'm not here to discuss the philosophy of science."

"We don't think the questions about your study are irrelevant," I said. "But let's change the subject. We know that this guy Corman contacted you the night before Connors' murder. We've analyzed his phone records." I had to say that, of course.

"Corman......Corman. Oh, you mean Jake. Very sad about his demise. Suicide is always tragic. I could have done something if he'd confided in me. He'd left a message where he seemed to be threatening suicide, but I checked my cell phone just too late."

In my view, Berryman wasn't exactly convincing. I'd dealt with conmen, drug dealers, and sex trade workers who presented with more sincerity than this man. Red thought it was just his arrogance.

"That's exactly who I mean," I said. "Jake Corman. So, what did you talk about?"

"I don't exactly recall..... let me see.... Yes, I remember. Jake did some odd job work for me. I was just seeing if he was available. It's hard to get work done these days at short notice."

"What sort of work?" said Red.

"I think it was for my theatre group. Look, I didn't know that Corman was a killer. I really didn't. He came to me a few months ago. He had lost his job because of Covid."

"You said theatre group. Which was one that?" I said.

"The Calgary Pro-Arte theatre group."

"The CPTG?" Red enquired.

"Exactly."

"We also know that you called Mrs. Connors the night before she was murdered."

"You know, I can't be sure of that, but if you say so. You seem to have all the answers," Berryman said.

"We're absolutely sure you did," I said. "What was that all about?"

"I just don't recall. I often talked to her."

"Why was that?" Red said.

"Well, for one. Our clinic out east was named after her."

"Is that all?" I said.

"We were both involved in theatre projects, especially CTPG. We have been involved for years in the arts. She provided considerable financial support to a lot of organizations. It must have been something to do with that."

"And your call to Lonnie Greene?" Now that was just a guess, and he could have denied it.

"Probably theatre business as well. He was one of our patrons just like Connors, but he was also providing promotion and financial support to MMC."

"You knew that there had been some doubts about your research," said Red. I knew he was trying to put Berryman on the defensive again.

"I think you've made that abundantly clear. Academic research is always faced with these problems. You might suspect there is an element of professional jealousy in all of this."

"The Securities Commission might think otherwise," I replied.

"What are you saying? I hope you have not spoken to these people." His sphincter seemed close to relaxing completely.

"We will be," said Red. "My wife has an appointment with them tomorrow." This was all bullshit, but no harm in ruffling a few feathers.

"This could be ruinous to our organization. This could be fatal to the Canadian arm of this group." Berryman didn't look angry, more depressed by this news. He was beginning to deflate like a punctured beach ball. "This means jobs for Canadians." He was scraping the barrel with this crap.

"Let me change the subject," said Red. "Did you have any fatalities in your clinical trial?"

"A strange question, sir, but I'll have to be honest. We did have a couple of people pass away."

"Very interesting, to say the least," I said.

"Sad but not as interesting as you think," Berryman replied. "They were in the control group. Pre-existing conditions that caused their deaths."

That ended that line of questioning in a hurry, but it was a message from the receptionist that really ended the conversation. She told him over the intercom that he was scheduled for a conference call with Mr. Greene. Berryman looked relieved as he ushered us out of the office.

I am not sure that we had made a great deal of progress with our meeting. But we went back to my place to discuss it. Jen was supposed to be meeting Bourne, so Red had a bit of spare time. It was about the time she was scheduled to call us back. But we'd give her a bit more time. We'd worried too much the last time and that, like most times, worry hadn't helped.

We had little to talk about until I received a text message from Arnold. He'd been able to investigate some of the financial details of MMC, especially the trading pattern of their stock. He'd done this complex statistical analysis. Arnold reckoned that they had set up a box to increase their share value. He had to explain a box to me. Person A buys and then sells to B, who pays more than A, who then sells it to C at a profit, and round and round it goes. It usually involves quite a few individuals or groups. The one name that he was able to retrieve was Lonnie Greene. I mentioned this to Red and told him that Greene was in a box. He added that he fucking well deserved to be.

So, we had compelling evidence that there was some financial chicanery going on. Greene was certainly involved, and Berryman and the MMC may have known about this. It was only when I handed the account details to Red that he noticed something more than startling. When he examined the list of client names, he recognized two of them. Kevin Sykes and Jake Sharples. Where had we seen those names before? They were the two suicide victims that had been found in their cars. There were also three other names on there we didn't recognize. I jotted down their names. There were two males and one female. Their files ended abruptly. It might mean nothing, but it would be interesting to identify them, and we did. It was more than interesting. Apart from our two victims, all three of the other individuals had been reported as having committed suicide in the previous two months. We couldn't immediately see how they had committed suicide. What we knew was that the box scam was using their names on phony accounts despite being dead, and they had all used the same brokerage house. Brockbanks. That house was owned by Lonnie Greene. We certainly had the goods on him now. The question was, how could we use it?

It was time to call it a day, but I did need to contact Arnold to see if he had any other information. I was able to do this through Daphne, who arrived back a few minutes later. Rita and her described a very satisfying day at the Food Bank, though my freeze-dried curries apparently got little attention. As my mother used to say. "Sidney, kids are starving in Biafra that would welcome this stuff." Perhaps, the Food Bank should send it there.

I mentioned to Daphne that Arnold should get in touch with me if he thought it necessary. She disappeared to make him dinner. I doubt she was thinking of the Macaroni Cheese that I got. I then tried to get hold of Louie to see if he could tell me any more about the names we had just discovered. I suppose they could have all frozen to death in their cars, but that was unlikely. But it would be nice to find out how they may have committed suicide.

Red tried to contact Jen, but there was no response. Perhaps it was a bad battery again, but it might be something more concerning. As I thought about where she was to meet Bourne, something dawned on me. Bourne had told me he didn't drive a car at all. He was a conservationist. So, what the fuck was Jen doing meeting him in the parking lot at North Hill Mall? It didn't seem to make sense. Bourne surely hadn't walked there to meet her. I hoped it eventually made sense.

I said nothing to Red as he left, but I had to, three hours later, when he called me. Jen had still not turned up and was not answering his calls. Although we'd had the problem the day before, her cell phone was now charged up. She'd never been out of touch for this long. Red was panicking. I couldn't blame him. It was a bit too early to contact the police and report her as missing. You had to wait for at least twenty-four hours. But it didn't stop me from getting hold of Louie. He said that he would be over in twenty minutes and suggested that Red be there as well. I called Red. He said he would be there in half an hour.

When Red arrived at our house, he was bordering somewhere between panic and paranoia. I had never seen him quite so compromised, but I doubt that I would have been any different. Time was always considered to be the essence when looking for a missing person. We had better sort this out quickly. The longer these situations went on, the worse the prognosis. Red knew this as well. I suggested it might be a good idea if Red slept in our spare room if he could.

CHAPTER 17

That evening was difficult. Louie came over and he had helped, but it was more a message of reassurance. He asked for a recent picture of Jen and her car registration and said that an all-points bulletin would be put out, but we were no nearer a resolution. He assured us she would be found. We knew that. You always found them eventually, but we didn't consider the most obvious question. The issue was who would have done this. In our view, it must have something to do with the Connors' case. Was this someone we didn't know? The most obvious candidate would have been Corman, but he was long since dead.

I couldn't think of anyone else we knew who would do this. Did Greene have any other nefarious contacts? He probably knew a few, but that didn't get us any further. Louie said he would check this out, but it would take time, time that we didn't have. It was as he left that he said that they had contacted the nearby mall and he was sure that there would be video surveillance tapes available as early as the following morning. He said that he would get back to us.

Red continued to call Jen's number until the early hours. He had no success, and we ruled out the flat battery hypothesis. Whoever had taken Jen had not contacted us to demand a ransom as they often did, but we concluded that this was not for the money, at least not directly. We surmised, perhaps hoped, that this was a move to deter us from going to the Securities Commission. That would not work, but whoever was involved couldn't possibly know this.

I think I managed about two hours of sleep until a phone call from Louie awakened me at about six. Red must have left in the middle of the night. Louie said that they had got the surveillance data from the shopping mall. He couldn't get it to us immediately but suggested that we should come down to the station later in the day. It was clear what had happened, he said. Jen had arrived at North Hill and parked her vehicle. After a few minutes, a small red saloon car drove up and parked next to her. It looked like a Fiat. You could see the driver; he was wearing a balaclava. Nothing necessarily suspicious about that. It was -25 and there was a stiff breeze. That could mean frostbite in minutes.

The guy wound down the window of his car and beckoned to her. Words were exchanged, and she then got in his car and they drove away. No violence was evident. But there was some key evidence. At least, it seemed so at first. The camera was able to pick out the license plate of the car. A check with vehicle records indicated that the owner lived in Beddington in the city's north. That was the good news. And the bad news. It had been stolen a few hours before. As Louie suggested, it probably would not take long before the police spotted this car. That did nothing to limit our anxiety and certainly did not help Red when I phoned him.

Rita was up early that morning. She made me a strong coffee and one of those packaged egg and sausage wraps. The ones you just heat. That was very thoughtful, but I knew as I took my first bite that trouble lay ahead. You see, I don't do very well with MSG. The problem is not immediate, but I can usually time it to make sure I am near facilities if you get my drift. Within three hours, I usually have to...... I think you can fill in the blanks. I was polite enough to eat it, but I sort of suggested that this was probably not a good idea for me in the near future.

I had just taken my last bite when there was a knock at the door. It was Arnold. He looked excited. This was unusual. He usually had a bit of a poker face. I invited him in and offered him an egg and sausage wrap. I was not being generous. I knew Rita would offer me the second one anytime soon. That would have led to my intestinal devastation. Fortunately, he accepted it. Probably good manners. I couldn't imagine Daphne giving him one of these.

It soon became apparent why Arnold was so enthusiastic. He typed out that he had cracked the MMC documents, and they certainly had a story to tell. He was able to find out that the public reporting of the clinical trial was bullshit. We were able to match up the coded names with the real names.

It seemed as if nine patients had died in the experimental group and none in the placebo. Berryman had been lying his arse off. Some patients had been released but were obviously quite ill. I found out that Rita was on the list, but she was listed as anomalous, whatever that meant. Now that I had the exact names, I could ask Louie about the cause of death. He could get that information quickly. I phoned him and he agreed to have that information available when he got to our place. We thought we knew exactly how two of them had died. We certainly knew where they were found. What had happened to the others?

I immediately called Red, and he still had heard nothing. I tried to reassure him, but he was way past that. I told him I was going to check out Greene later in the day. He was up to his armpits in this shit. Red could join us to look at the surveillance tape, but that would be about it. I reckoned he was not in any shape to be doing anything else. But as far as Greene was concerned, I wasn't about to go into the lion's den on my own. You just never knew. I had an idea. I asked Arnold if he would join me when I went to see Greene. It took about two nanoseconds for him to nod in agreement. His support would make me feel a lot more comfortable. This was more for his mental abilities and not his physical capability, but given what I suspected to be his background, you never knew.

We agreed to meet at two o'clock. He still had plenty of time to examine the copied files and he would spend the morning doing this.

As he left, Rita emerged from the kitchen and asked me what Arnold had found out. I told her in detail. I reminded her she was considered anomalous by MMC. She didn't know what that meant either, but then she hit me with a bit of a bombshell. Well, it would have been more of a bombshell if she had told me this two days earlier. Remember, she told us that she thought she recognized Sharples, the second apparent suicide. She had. He was the guy in the next room at the clinic, the one that was looking rather ill. I mean, this didn't come as a surprise, but it was beginning to confirm my suspicions about the whole situation.

As I left to go down to the police station to see Louie, I also thought of something that had been lingering in the back of my mind for a few days. When I had neatly been caught in the operating room at the clinic, I assumed that the security guard had been thick not to be concerned about an apparently dead body in front of him. Perhaps the reason was that he was used to dead bodies in the clinic. If that was so, it would hardly be a surprise to him, though to be fair, corpses typically didn't fart.

When I arrived at the police station, both Red and Louie were waiting for me. We went into Louie's office. The videotape was just as he had described, but that doesn't mean that it was not interesting. I had met Bourne, and I knew what he looked like. While the build of the character in the video was similar, it just didn't look like him. I remembered that he had mentioned that he said that he didn't drive. If this was him, then he obviously did drive to the shopping centre. But why would he lie? Red quickly left, which gave me the chance to question Louie. Red said that he would continue to try to get hold of Jen. But as we say in the trade, he was pissing in the wind. Her cell phone battery would have long run out. The situation was now more than a crisis.

When I got Louie alone, I asked if it was possible to examine Corman's body. He said that would be difficult, if not impossible, at least in the short term. That didn't stop me from asking a key question. Did the body that had been fished out of the river have the word 'peace' tattooed on the knuckles of the right hand? He said that he couldn't answer that but would make a phone call to find out. He said that the body had been identified and that he thought I was looking for something that just wasn't there.

I had arranged to meet with Arnold shortly after lunch, but I first had to contact Greene and let him know we were coming to see him. We would not take no for an answer. It didn't come to that after I told him we were due to meet the Securities Commission the next day. He said he would be expecting me in the next hour. That was easy. Perhaps he had something to tell me. I told him that I would be bringing my associate with me. I stressed that Arnold was completely deaf, but that he was my driver and confidant. I didn't mention the word witness.

When I got home, Arnold was waiting for me with more interesting news. He had found a letter from Berryman to Greene. Berryman said that he was very disturbed about Connors' death and hoped that Greene and that fucktard Corman were not involved. Fucktard. Not the sort of language you would expect from a distinguished doctor. Although I still disliked Berryman, I was impressed that he could use the language of the streets. While the letter could have been a cover for his guilt, it seemed to suggest that Berryman may not have been responsible. The highway of guilt was looking as if it went straight through Lonnie Greene, at least for now.

Bel-Aire is a rather salubrious area of Calgary. Not actually my description. I got that from Wikipedia. I then had to look up the meaning of the word salubrious. It means healthy and wholesome. Not that I would suggest that if Lonnie Greene was in its midst. I knew that the crime rate for the area was described as being 60% lower than the Calgary average. I had a feeling that was about to take a hit.

I decided we would go in the company truck. Remember, the Imperial Ex-terminators truck. With sandbags in the back, it behaved better than anything else on the ice and snow. It looked a bit out of place in Bel-Aire and the very sight of it might have dropped property values by 2-3%. When we found Greene's place, I had to be impressed. It was very sizable and imposing with a triple garage and plenty of parking spaces and fake marble pillars in front of the house.

I was surprised that Greene answered the door himself. People like Greene usually employ someone to do that. He invited us into his office. It was opulent. I know, I had to look that up as well. It was all leather and pictures. Most of the pictures were of established stars of screen and stage, with a few sports stars thrown in. They were all autographed.

Greene's small talk was limited, and he got straight to the point.

"So nice to meet you, Mr. Arbuckle. Now what the fuck is all this shite about the Securities Commission?"

I explained that we had had preliminary discussions with them and that we would be meeting again the following morning. He did not look at all pleased.

"Do you pricks know just who you are dealing with?" he said.

"I think we do," I replied. "But we would like to hear your side of the story. Our meeting is scheduled for tomorrow."

"There is a lot of money and power involved here," he said. "When people cross money and power, it can be very dangerous?"

"Are you threatening us?" I said. It seemed such a stupid comment. Of course, he was trying to scare the shit out of us.

He then spent several minutes telling us about the misfortunes of those who had crossed him. There were a few famous names in there who had apparently committed suicide. I was beginning to get a bit bored by his conversation. Let's face it. He could only kill us one way, and I doubted he would hesitate if he thought he could get away with it. It wouldn't be now. These guys employ people to do the dirty work.

It was then I began to feel the wrath of the egg and sausage wrap from a few hours before. It didn't slowly develop. The wave hit you all at once and that once was now. I just had to go. It seemed odd. in the face of his barrage of threats, that it wasn't his implied threats that might have had the laxative effect on me. I was made of sterner stuff, though not stern enough to overcome MSG.

I meekly asked him if I could use the bathroom. He looked exasperated, but he would look a lot more exasperated if he didn't tell me where the bathroom was. He told me it was down the corridor. I couldn't miss it. Of course, I didn't intend to. He also suggested that Arnold sit in the corridor while he made a phone call. I ushered Arnold out of the room. As I was leaving, my cell phone went off. It was someone who was trying to sell me another 3,000 television channels.

"Yes, inspector," I exclaimed. "I'm with Mr. Greene right now. Just routine stuff. I'll call you later." I made sure that Greene heard us. The guy on the other end must have been very confused. He must have thought I was taking the piss, but I was just safeguarding myself.

One thing that the uninitiated tend to forget is that while people might be deaf, some deaf people can be very good at lip-reading. Arnold was not only capable of his lip reading, he was an expert at it. Unfortunately for Greene, he didn't realize this. He picked up the phone and began a conversation without realizing that Arnold, who was sitting at least thirty feet away, was deciphering every word. When I returned from the bathroom, I walked back into Greene's office and sat down. There wasn't much else to say. He'd given us a warning. We'd received it. It was up to us to take notice or not.

Once I got back from the toilet, Arnold was giving out vibes that we should leave. Not sure what they were, but I certainly picked something up. We made our exit quickly. I'd never seen Arnold agitated before. He just wasn't that sort of guy, but he obviously would have to wait until we got home to tell me what was bothering him. Just before we arrived home, Louie called me to tell me that Corman had a tattoo that said 'peace' on the fingers of his right hand. That told me everything I wanted to know. That wasn't Corman who had died. It was Bourne. Corman must have paid someone to play his sister and identify him.

Sadly, this could only mean one thing. Corman had Jen. I decided I would keep my supposition to myself. I suspected Red would freak out if he found out.

When we got home, Arnold typed frantically on his tablet. What he had to say was chilling. When I was detained in the bathroom, Greene had made a phone call. Although Arnold was not in the room, he could read Greene's lips. Thank goodness Greene wasn't wearing a mask. He didn't get everything, but Greene had said something about putting plans on hold and not doing anything drastic. And then he said, "Don't harm the girl." But Arnold was not completely sure. What he was sure about was the gun that he had seen secreted between books on the bookcase. Perhaps it was a mock gun, but you never knew. And there was still no word about Jen.

I called Louie with an update. He said that there was an APB out for Corman. There wasn't much I could do that afternoon. I sat by the phone. I stopped biting my nails when I was a spotty adolescent. I had just started again.

It was at that point we decided it might be time to use my credit card to investigate Greene further. Remember, I could open most doors with my credit card. I knew Greene would be out tonight. He would be attending a wine and cheese party for the MMC sharehold-ers. I knew this because Rita and I had been invited. I suppose that was protocol, but Rita and I would not be attending. We didn't drink wine and cheese gave me gas.

We decided to take a look around after eight 'o'clock. The wine and cheese reception was scheduled to begin at 7.30 PM. I was not sure what we might find at Greene's, and I hoped the house didn't have electronic surveillance. If it did, at this point, I didn't give Jack Shit. Since I thought it likely that he was renting the house, the chances were good that it didn't have cameras. I arranged with Arnold to meet that evening.

I spent the afternoon doing paperwork, but my mind was not on it. I knew Jen was in real danger. Corman had killed before and probably wouldn't hesitate to do it again. We could only hope that Greene's conversation was with Corman and that he would resist any violent behaviour. I didn't pretend that he would continue to do so.

When I met Arnold later that evening, he had one suggestion. He felt that turning up at Greene's house in the Imperial Ex-terminators truck would not be a good idea. It would identify us all too easily. Neighbours always seem to notice that sort of thing. He suggested we go in a car that would fit the surroundings better. He suggested Daphne's Jaguar, but she would have to drive. Sounded like a great idea to me. It would sure save me some gas money.

We left at eight 'o'clock and reached Bel-Aire shortly after that. I hadn't travelled in such a classy car for years. The car had real leather seats. When we arrived at Greene's house, it was in darkness. I got my credit card out, but it just didn't work, and part of the reason was the fact that there was a combination on the lock. I imagined that would be it, but Arnold took out this gadget from his pocket and within seconds we were in. No dogs, no maid, no cameras, or at least none that we were aware of. Our COVID-19 masks sort of hid our identities.

Everything was going according to plan. We went into Greene's office. I looked around at the desk to see if there was anything incriminating. Not really, except I was able to find Greene's chequebook and in it, there were two checks written to Corman for the sum of fifteen thousand dollars. One was dated two days after Connors' death and the second just a few days ago.

There was also a stack of business files dealing with other companies on the stock exchange. There was a safe in the corner of the room, but it was unlikely that even Arnold could work out the combination in a couple of minutes. Arnold seemed to take an age examining the gun, but I reckoned he knew what he was doing. I saw him taking some things from a bag that he was carrying. What for? I had no idea. I also looked at Greene's appointment book. He had scribbled, 'What to do with Arbuckle? Meet Berryman at the CPTG warehouse tomorrow at 2:00 p.m. Will have to deal with him.' What the fuck was that all about?

It was easy in these sorts of situations to misjudge the time and be caught. It had happened once before. Daphne sounded the car horn after thirty minutes, so we knew it was time to leave. I am not completely sure that we achieved much, though it was becoming increasingly clear that Greene was front and centre of all the malfeasance. Once we were home, I contacted Red and then Louie. They had no news. Even I was beginning to panic.

As I lay in bed, I received a call from Louie. It was late, but he had some very interesting information for me. He had tracked down the cause of death for the nine patients who had dropped out of the trial. Five, including our two deaths, committed suicide. It was an unexplained car accident or suicide by poisoning. Several of the others died of other diseases which could not be linked to the trial. Two of them were diagnosed with COVID-19, the new mutant variety. Their death certificate had been signed by Dr. Berryman. It was easy to see how the clinic had falsified their data. If they had not been screwed by Bourne's article focusing on the statistics, they certainly were now.

It didn't take me long to doze off, but before I did, I decided it might be worthwhile to pay a visit to the CPTG warehouse the next day. Greene was about to meet with Berryman. It would be interesting to be a fly on the wall.

I spent a restless night thinking about Jen. I knew that worrying would not help a bit. Still, I couldn't help it. I stole one of Rita's sleeping pills. It gave me a couple of hours of bad dreams.

CHAPTER 18

When your phone rings at 7.30 in the morning, it is usually the wrong number. This was not and thank god it wasn't. An unusual comment for me, but in times of crisis you'll hang on to anything. Red had received a phone call from Jen. She was safe, but only just. Obviously, her cell phone battery must have been completely discharged by now, but she came up with a trick to resolve that issue.

But I'm jumping to the end of the story. Jen, who was now being checked out at the Foothills Hospital, had gone to meet Bourne at North Hill and, much against her better judgment, had gotten into the red car. Not like her, I suppose, but I guess we all make mistakes. He had immediately pulled a gun on her, and she realized pretty quickly that she was sitting next to Corman. They drove around for a while, though she had no idea where. He had made her put on a balaclava and covered up the eye holes. Eventually, he shepherded her into a house. She guessed it was in the north. Something she had always had. An amazing sense of direction. He took off the balaclava, and she was pushed down a flight of stairs. Corman unlocked a padlock and shoved her into a sparsely furnished bedroom. There were no windows.

The room was furnished with a small chair and a bed. There was one blanket. and precious little heat except for a small inadequate heater. There was a small unshaded light bulb, a battery-powered table lamp and that was it. He forgot to take her cell phone away from her. Corman bolted the door. There was no easy way out.

Over the next couple of days, she was isolated and given a couple of sandwiches to keep her going. Corman was hardly seen but when he was, he had become increasingly irritated and mumbled that he would have to find a solution one way or another. Then he made a fatal mistake, though I, for one, would have not seen this coming. When he was giving her some food, he found her cell phone but tossed it on the floor, commenting that it would be flat and that it wouldn't work in the basement. He was right. But he had underestimated Jen's ingenuity.

One thing that Jen had noticed was that there were some bare water pipes that she could see through the ceiling tiles. She stood on the bed and could reach up to them. They were hot water pipes. Fortunately, Corman had kept the furnace going strong and the hot water was very hot. In my early days, I used to extend the length of batteries in my transistor radio by heating them slowly in the oven. Some days that worked and some days it didn't. On this occasion, she placed the battery on top of one of the pipes and wrapped it with some material. She would be eternally grateful that Corman had decided to continue heating the house and especially thankful that she had turned her phone off just before she handed it to Corman. That way, the battery had not been completely depleted. Almost, but not quite. Brilliant wasn't it? Except it wasn't. It didn't work.

Remember I mentioned Jen's ingenuity, That sort of stuff just doesn't disappear and she wasn't about to give up. She noticed that the desk lamp had a battery in it that was still functional. She was able to strip some wires and attach the lamp battery to the phone battery. Don't ask me just how she did it. She did tell me but I would fuck it up if you asked me to describe it. It worked and the rest is history.

It was just before daybreak when she was convinced that Corman would be asleep when she inserted the battery into the phone and called Red. Since he was hardly sleeping these days, he heard it go off right away, and she just had enough power left to tell him she thought she was in the basement of a house in the northwest. What that was based on, I never found out, but Red worked it out right away. He'd been to Corman's house and knew exactly where to go. He called the police, but by then he was already on his way. I don't know whether Corman was planning to leave but by the time Red got to the house by Confederation Park, Corman was just leaving in the stolen red car.

Corman would not be a problem for now. Hopefully, the police would track him down. Red smashed his way into the house and ran downstairs before flattening the bedroom door with his shoulder. After that, Red thought it would be wise to get her to the hospital for a checkup. I'm glad to say that she was in relatively good shape, with no apparent issues with her baby.

It was time for her to take it easy for a few days. Red should have done the same, but he was intent on finding Corman and so were the police. Within the hour, they had found the red car parked by the Calgary Winter Club up by Nose Hill with footprints heading away up the hill. I should add that they were size eight with the same tread that was seen at Connors' house.

We had spotted his truck there before in several locations. I wondered what his affinity for Nose Hill was. The police blocked off all exits to the park within the hour, but there was simply no sign of him. He easily could have slipped away at any point of the park's perimeter.

We checked the Winter Club, but there was no sign of him around there. It was also possible that he had another vehicle parked close to the park and escaped in that. It was up to the police now. We wouldn't be involved in the search directly from now on. The police assured us they would find him, and they did eventually, but not in a place they could ever have expected.

This was a cause for celebration, though it was difficult to go wild at that time in the morning. I had one of those newfangled coffees and tried to pretend that it was the potential highlight of my day. It didn't matter. Jen had been found and now we had to wrap this whole business up. We now knew more about what had happened, but as they say, we would have to seal the deal.

I texted Arnold and suggested we might have a look-see at the CPTG studio space. Remember. Things were starting to go my way. Greene had indicated that he was going to meet Berryman at two. I suspected I could use my credit card with no trouble at all to get in. I invited Arnold over for a breakfast bite. When I told Rita, she served her much-vaunted bacon sandwich. Served crispy, it was nirvana for me. Unfortunately, Arnold only ate the bread. I was later to find out that he was a vegetarian. Still, it meant that I got a double serving. Everything was going my way.

We decided we would get to the studio space before lunch. We knew that Berryman and Greene were due to meet later that afternoon and though it would have been great to be a fly on the wall, the dangers of being there in my view probably outweighed the advantages. After all, Greene possessed a gun, and, if cornered, he would undoubtedly not hesitate to use it. This time we had no problems using the truck to get there, though we would not park it too close to the studio.

The CPTG studio was tucked away in one of the industrial estates in the northeast. While it was mainly used for storage, it was fully capable of putting on plays in its space. You could only squeeze about sixty people in their little theatre but since the Covid outbreak, you really couldn't squeeze anybody in there legally.

Breaking in wasn't difficult. I mean, the real issue was that there would be nothing of value in there to steal. So why use triple locks? Most of these places were stuffed with sets and props. These were of little value to most people unless you thought there was some long-term value in a rotary dial phone, or a 13th-century crossbow bow made from an old coat hanger. It was probably, for this reason, that there was minimal security. Once we had opened the front door, we entered the foyer. This was adorned with pictures of CPTG actors who had made good. I had not heard of any of them, but then I probably couldn't have named more than five living actors. Now down to four. Sean Connery had just died.

At the end of the corridor was something labelled the green room. There was no truth in advertising. It was painted purple. This was apparently where the actors would meet to get changed and await their cues to go on stage. Adjoining this was a door that clearly led to the props room. This was padlocked, but this was no barrier to Arnold. When we walked into the props room, we faced a desk and chair. It was surrounded by row upon row of props, some big, some small. The smaller items were in labelled boxes. The desk had a notice fixed to the front. It said, "Keep your fucking hands in your pockets. All props must be signed for." It was signed with Corman's name.

It was what we found on the desk that was the most intriguing. There were a couple of checks for several thousand dollars written to Corman from Harith Investments. I suspect this was one of Greene's shell companies and Arnold was soon able to confirm this. We also found reams and reams of Basildon Bond paper sitting on the shelf. It did look expensive but I'm sure they must have got it in a cheap job lot of this stuff somewhere. I can't imagine where they got 15 boxes of this stuff, but let's face it. Who was using writing paper these days?

There was also an entire stack of brown-tinted pill bottles we had seen with the first suicide. It was clear that Corman had printed false labels and stuck them on the pill bottles. Why he had not taken the CPTG label off is difficult to say. Perhaps he thought all pill bottles needed a label like this. There were also a couple of hypodermic syringes sitting on the desk and a bottle of something called potassium chloride. I had come across that somewhere else, but at the time I just couldn't recall where. There was also something else electronic sitting on a shelf behind the desk. It made little sense to me, but it made sense to Arnold. Apparently, it was some sort of gizmo that allowed you to break into just about any car. Just about everything else had a slight dusty veneer. Clearly, the police would have to see this, so we were very careful not to leave any fingerprints.

We carefully locked everything up and decided to have a look around the rest of the studio. There was apparently a show that must have been in production when the pandemic struck. The theatre did not re-open, and the seats had been rolled back to reveal a couple of mousetraps that were now fully occupied.

Overlooking the stage was a sound and lights booth. Probably nothing in there that could be of much interest, but you never knew. Nothing ventured, nothing gained. We climbed up a steel ladder behind the booth. There was no need to put the light on. The light from the stage illuminated the booth. It was a good job that it did. We had been messing around in there for about five minutes when I suddenly became aware of Greene walking into the theatre space. I tugged on Arnold to stoop down. I slid to the back of the booth. I was sure that he couldn't see us, though I could see him. He walked towards the booth and shouted up to see if anybody was in the booth. He noticed one of the mousetraps, kicked it under the seats, and decided not to come up. Seconds later, the theatre door opened, and in walked Berryman. Shit, they had obviously changed the time of their meeting,

Greene was obviously in no mood for a pleasant get-together. The first clue was when he pulled the pistol out of his pocket and told Berryman to sit down by a table on the stage.

"Greene, I hope this is some sort of joke," said Berryman.

"Dr. Berryman, I never joke when I'm holding a gun."

We were having a little difficulty hearing. I hadn't thought of this, but Arnold had. There was a microphone that relayed sound up to the booth. He turned it on and gave me a set of earphones. Now everything was clear to me, though, of course, not to Arnold.

"So, what the fuck are you pointing it at me for?"

"It's called elimination of all possible loose ends. I thought I would have to eliminate Corman, but I can't find the fucker. But when I do, he'll deserve his fate. He was, let us say, looking after a female inconvenient this morning. The dickwad let her escape."

"Just a minute. I thought Corman was fished out of the river. I thought he offed himself. I received a message from him. He sounded depressed."

"You believed the police story. That's funny," Greene said. "Bourne was threatening to bring down the whole house of cards and this Jen woman would have done the same."

"She interviewed one of my nurses, so I know who she is," he replied.

"We couldn't risk his story being published and certainly didn't want anybody talking to the Securities Commission. It was him who was fished out of the river."

"What about the girl? What was that about?"

"I gave Corman the job of looking after her and he screwed up. He kidnapped her because she knew the truth and was threatening to go to the authorities. She worked for Lou Diamond Investigations, some wannabe private eye. She was the brains, if you ask me."

I was tempted to open the window and tell him to fuck off, but Arnold held me back. Besides, sometimes the truth hurts.

"Why would I do anything to harm you, Greene? It would only harm me. Just be logical."

"Look Larry, old boy......you only know half the story."

"Meaning?" said Berryman.

"I'm a businessman and I have to do some unpleasant things. You, scientists, are there to be scientists except, of course, when you are manipulating the data".

"I admit to that. It was a stupid thing to do. It could...no, it will finish my academic career, I suppose."

"So, I and my associates were left to do the dirty work. Connors could have blown this whole thing up. We had to get rid of her and I just had the man to do it. Corman was not cheap, but it had to be done. Besides, what is a few thousand dollars when we are talking millions, possibly billions, in profits?"

"I didn't know you were behind that. I had my suspicions, I admit," said Berryman.

"And now you know. You see, we were what you might call protection for the project. Somebody had to get rid of all the bodies.

And we did. If they died, they committed suicide. If they were harmed by your medication but were still alive, they were criminally removed from the equation."

"And pray tell me, how they did that?" said Berryman.

"I suppose you could say we vaccinated them with potassium chloride."

"You bastards. You injected them with potassium chloride. That's fatal. It precipitates cardiac failure. And it's difficult to spot with a rudimentary autopsy. Nobody would be looking for it."

"Exactly, and then we made it look like suicide. Two frozen bodies. It was all so easy. Nobody realized what we were doing until Connors began to twig it. How the hell were we supposed to know her father was involved in the trial? And why the fuck did she take out life insurance on the old guy? I can tell you why. It was greed,"

"So, you killed her."

"I didn't, but Mr. Corman was very good at this sort of thing or, at least, he said he was. He made some stupid mistakes, and the police fingered him for the crime. Corman may border on stupidity, but I doubt that he will ever be caught. Besides the police, who are even stupider than Corman, actually think he is dead."

"Weren't you worried about the press finding out?"

"Not really. Most of the big corporations control the mass media. Those guys tell you what they think you need to know."

"What about Bourne?"

"A bit of a loose cannon. He had to be controlled."

"How was he killed?"

"You know I hate that word killed. I prefer eliminated."

"So, how was he eliminated?"

"Well, we had to make it seem as if it was Corman who had died. The rest was easy. A blow to the back of the head, an injection of potassium chloride, and then thrown into the river. Pity he fell onto the ice where he might be easily found. Otherwise, he would have been an anonymous corpse found floating in the river somewhere near Medicine Hat."

"Corman must have had help to do this."

"I don't ask unnecessary questions. Not my business. The less you know about these things, the better."

"I guess you are going to kill me. You think you'll get away with this?"

"Of course, I do, Dr. Berryman. I'll try to make it look like suicide. Shouldn't be difficult." There will be a note on Basildon Bond writing paper, I thought to myself.

"And what will you do?"

"I'll probably be on the TV extolling the virtues of MMC and shedding a few tears for our medical director...he was such a good man. So diligent, so conscientious. We can never replace him, except we will."

With that, Greene advanced towards Berryman and pumped four bullets into him. He didn't hesitate. Berryman stood there for a second before collapsing on the ground. He looked very dead. Greene still had two bullets left in that gun.

CHAPTER 19

We kept silent for a couple of minutes before climbing down the ladder and attending to the body. Greene seemed to have spent a couple of minutes in the props room. When he left, we immediately bent down over Berryman. There was a surprising lack of blood. There was one simple reason for this. Berryman was not dead. He was not even injured. As Berryman rose from the floor, Arnold pointed to his tablet. He had written, "When I was in Greene's house, I made sure he was shooting blanks."

"What the fuck were you two doing in here?" Berryman said.

"No point biting the hand that feeds you," I replied. "Let's say we were just extending our investigation."

"What did you hear?" he said.

"All of it," I replied. As I said that, Arnold nudged me. He had recorded the whole interaction on his tablet. Berryman realized what he had done.

Suddenly, the arrogant Larry Berryman did not look so arrogant after all. In fact, he looked completely deflated. Just to prove his point, Arnold pressed a button on his tablet and you could hear most of the conversation, especially after the speaker had been turned on in the booth.

"What are you going to do about this?" said Berryman.

"Well, we obviously will have to report this to the police. What you do about the finagling of the research data is completely up to you, but if I were you, I would come clean about the whole affair," I replied. This seemed to make Berryman even more despondent.

"Would it be O.K. to leave?" he asked. I could do with a stiff drink.

I pointed to the exit. No real need to keep him. I think he was actually unaware of what Greene had been doing. I suspect he chose not to think about it. I think psychologists call it denial. You have to think like a killer in these cases and Berryman obviously hadn't.

We locked up the Space and climbed into the truck. The first thing we did was to contact Louie with our news. Clearly, the plan would be to find Greene as soon as possible. He still had a gun with two bullets in it. If he was cornered, he wouldn't hesitate to use those bullets. We couldn't be completely sure the remaining bullets were blanks. I expected that the police would have no trouble finding him. But as usual, I was wrong. They tended to look in all the wrong places.

When we got home, we sat on the sofa and turned on the television. We wanted to see what was going on with the MMC stock price. It was still doing well, but we were shocked to see Greene on live TV extolling the virtues of Xyloleptokinase aka Radishon. He was quite impressive, as many stock promoters tend to be. But appearing on TV after you have just killed somebody really took balls. I thought that at that moment, Greene would be quickly picked up. But again, I was wrong.

A few minutes later, Red and Jen turned up. Jen looked none the worse for wear and could talk dispassionately about her experience with Corman. She described him as the prototypical psychopath, but I reckon we had already worked that out. He hadn't talked much and, in fact, gave her the impression that she was simply being used as a bargaining ploy. She knew that the truth was probably more negative than this. We didn't linger on the subject.

Red had two interesting pieces of news. On his way to our house, he had heard a news bulletin about an hour after the TV appearance that the police were looking for Lonnie Greene, a person of interest who might have been involved in a suspicious death at the CPTG space earlier in the day. This was, of course, a lie and I can only speculate why they had said this. Perhaps they thought that if they said Berryman was still alive it would definitely prompt Greene to go on the run. After all, Berryman could implicate Greene not only in attempted murder but the whole affair with MMC. It didn't make sense to me, but the police had their methods. I doubted he would be easily caught if he heard that on the radio, and, as it turned out, he wasn't easily caught.

The second piece of news was much more exciting. When Jen visited the hospital, they ran a series of tests to make sure that her pregnancy was going as expected. It wasn't. The latest scan indicated that she was expecting twins. This was great news for them, and Rita went apeshit about it. She even started suggesting names, but at this time they had not determined the sexes, so it was all a bit redundant. Rita was doing so much better and was back to her old self. Rat poison and her seemed to have got on very well.

Red said that they would be having a restful evening and that he had bought a couple of tickets to Vancouver. He thought that both of them needed a bit of rest and recreation and he was right. I offered to give them a lift to the airport the following morning.

Later that afternoon, Louie called me and mentioned that they had tried to get Greene at his house, but he was not there and was apparently on the run. Louie again assured me it would not take long to find him. They would be monitoring all means of transport out of Calgary. When I told him about Jen's pregnancy, he became very excited and said he would be over later with a bottle of tuica to toast the news. I would have to make sure he didn't make Jen drink this stuff. Even sniffing that stuff could be fatal to the fetuses.

I knew there was going to be some bad news on the financial front. It was fairly obvious that the shares in MMC would be severely impacted by the news filtering out. Our investment would be worthless at the end of the day. I knew the stock market was a bit like gambling at a casino, so we had only ever treated the possibility of financial gain with some amusement. Of course, as Red pointed out, people like Greene would win whatever happened. He had almost certainly shorted the stock through one of his many companies. So, if the stock dropped dramatically, he would still make a massive profit.

It was clear that our involvement was ending. We met that night to agree on exactly what had happened. Many people had been hurt one way or another and the hurt would continue in a way that I could not have predicted. We were just toasting Jen's good news when Red received a phone call from Dave Jessop.

He was at the MMC clinic. He was more than upset because I could hear him bellowing across the room. It seemed that he had been doing his rounds and gone into Berryman's office. Although he rarely did this, he had gone into the operating theatre and found Berryman's body there. This was obviously a suicide... a real one. This time there was no note on Basildon Bond paper and no empty bottle of pills, but a later postmortem showed he had injected himself with potassium chloride. It would have been a quick death. I was not surprised that he did this.

In a way, this course of events was not completely surprising. Berryman's career was over, and he knew it. Overcoming the exposure and shame would have been difficult for him. As a researcher, he would be treated as a pariah. I knew this would be difficult, if not impossible, for him to deal with. I don't think the truth ever really came out and there was eventually a memorial in his name. Apparently, there was a bit of a cover-up by the medical profession. As Red pointed out, we always look after our own.

This put a bit of a damper on our celebrations, but it did not stop Louie from getting slightly hammered on tuica. When he became tipsy, you couldn't shut him up. He obviously couldn't drive, and Daphne, who lived in the same neighbourhood as Louie, offered to give him a lift home. Arnold was quite amused by this and said via his tablet that Daphne could always turn her hearing aid off.

I slept soundly that night. It was the first time I had done this in quite a while. As the minutes ticked towards midnight, I realized that our contract with Mrs. Connors was due to expire in a few minutes.

We had done our best for her and I think we had succeeded. It would not go down in the annals of crime-fighting, but we had done our job and I'm sure Connors would have appreciated it. Even so, she was far from blameless for this whole affair.

When I woke the next morning, the weather had taken a definite turn for the worse. A high-pressure cell from the Yukon had settled over Southern Alberta and the temperatures had fallen into the minus thirties. Although I had, for once, plugged in my block heater, I wasn't at all sure that the Ex-terminator would start. Red and Jen arrived shortly after breakfast and after a quick coffee, I went outside to start the truck. I'll be blunt about this. It was fucking cold. Your skin would freeze in a couple of minutes if you lingered too long outside. And I didn't have a heater in the truck. Or did I. When I turned it on, it worked. I found out later that Rita had taken it in for repairs and now I had a heater. I mean, isn't that what wives are for? I went back inside and left the heater on for twenty minutes until it was toasty warm. We were in no real hurry, and as we drove to the airport, we passed the east side of Nose Hill. It was covered in snow and a heavy mist covered the top. At that moment, I couldn't have realized how close I was to Corman.

I would usually drop people off at the airport and be on my way, but this time I thought I would wave them off at the gate. I'd left my car running in the drop-off zone, but there was nobody around. I'd pop out every twenty minutes, do a loop, and repark.

We were two hours early, and you needed some of that time going through the rigmarole of checking in and security. Since the Covid business developed, you had to prove that you didn't have the disease. In order to prove that, there was a mandatory test you had to take. I knew Louie would definitely have passed. No virus could have survived the tuica.

I hoped there would not be a problem, especially since Jen was pregnant. We would have to wait about twenty minutes for the results. In the old days, flights to Vancouver would be overbooked.

But not this time. Only ten people were waiting to board, including a cop who seemed to be more interested in the stock market report that was available on the overhead TV screen. Perhaps he was invested in MMC. The group comprised a Sikh family, a couple of hockey players, a trio of giggling college students, and a grumpy old fart who was being difficult. He was in a wheelchair and wrapped in a blanket. He appeared to be completely bald, though he did have a sparse moustache. He wore wire glasses and was being pushed by an assistant. This guy was not impressed with being tested. I thought I knew him, but at my age, I thought I knew so many people, but I was usually wrong.

Eventually, the results were available, and Red and Jen were ushered to the desk. Within moments, they were through the gate and I was waving them goodbye. They deserved the rest, and I wouldn't be using Red for at least a week. Everyone else passed through until the old fart was the only one remaining. Unfortunately, there was bad news for him. He had failed the test. This did not go down at all well. At his age, Covid could kill him. He began to shout at the airline staff, but he didn't calm down when they threatened to call the police. Our cop had disappeared. It was only when they threatened him for the last time that they addressed him by name. "This is your last warning, Mr. Greene." Holy shit. This was Lonnie Greene, but it sure didn't look like him. Gone were his long, flowing black locks. Must have been a wig. And where the fuck did the moustache come from? Then I realized he must have gotten them from the props room at CPTG. I didn't see any cops around, but as he turned to leave, remarkably not in the wheelchair anymore, I confronted him.

"You're going nowhere, Greene," I said. He seemed to have a different idea and pulled out his gun. Now, I reckon he had not twigged the fact that he was shooting blanks, or were they? I decided to be ballsy though there was always the chance, it would be the last time I did that.

"I'm not afraid to use this,' he said. "I've used this before." Well, I was quite aware of that.

"So, fucking use it," I replied. And he did. He was only about three feet away, and I knew I could still be badly injured. When he shot, it didn't feel too bad. I was still alive, and so was Greene. Thank god the police had described a suspicious death. He assumed the bullets were real.

As I got up off the floor, I could see that he was sprinting down towards the entrance. A few people watched from the Tims coffee shop. I suspect they thought they were watching a movie. When Greene reached the main doors with me in a rather cold pursuit, he went for the nearest vehicle. Mine. I had left the keys in the ignition and the engine was running. He jumped in and attempted to make his getaway. He floored it and shot forward rather dramatically before the engine spluttered and stopped. The airbag was immediately deployed, and he was temporarily trapped in the vehicle. I knew what had happened. At least, I think I did. It was something about flooding the carburetor. That thing was not going to start again for a little while. It didn't have to. Within seconds, it was surrounded by police. Perhaps they had been watching from Tims. Greene was dragged away by the cops. I am not sure they knew who they had, but they soon would.

I must admit, I was in a state of shock. I talked to one of the security blokes outside, fully expecting a ticket, but he was decent about it. Told me to forget about a ticket and to get a coffee at Tims. I lingered over it and after a few minutes, Louie appeared. He looked worse than I did. Later, I found out there was only one decent security bloke at the airport. I got three tickets that day from the other guy.

Ten minutes later, Louie arrived.

"Heh, buddy," Louie said, grimacing. "Fucked up head.... tuica..... I buy coffee"

He was very impressed by what I had done and admitted he wouldn't have risked it. And he had some other very pertinent news. He said that Corman had been found.

"He big stiff," he said.

"I know that," I replied. "He's an asshole."

"No, no ...very big stiff.....ice-cold stiff." I thought we'd had this conversation once before.

I won't bore you with Louie's attack on the English language, but what Louie was trying to tell me was that Corman's body had been found. Not many people know this, but there are a couple of small caves in Nose Hill Park. Just big enough for one person. Corman must have known this and hidden out there for days. He had a small burner in there and plenty of blankets to keep warm. The only problem was the temperature had dropped to -38 degrees over the last 36 hours and that just was not survivable by anybody. His heater had failed. It was quite clear why we had found his vehicle by the Winter Club and why he had never been caught or even spotted. It was simply by chance that hikers had run across the cave, though what they were doing there in such temperatures is difficult to imagine.

It was ironic really that Corman had been found frozen in a thin veneer of ice. This was how it had all started. We found out that he was so frozen that it had been difficult to extract him from the cave right away. Fortunately, the next day a chinook blew in, which made the extraction easier.

When I got home, Louie picked up his car and left Rita and me alone. I had not had any private time with her for some time. I saw Arnold and Daphne on the way in, and I'm sure they felt the same way. They would probably spend the evening watching that new Korean movie with subtitles. I would sit down with Rita and we'd probably be watching reruns of Dancing with the Stars. Red and Jen would be sitting in a five-star hotel watching the sunset behind Vancouver Island. We would all be happy.

CHAPTER 20

It is often said that it is who you know, not what you know, that counts in life. This is largely true, and the legal proceedings seemed to prove this. There were two elements left in this case. What would happen to Greene and what would happen to MMC? Greene could afford a very fancy legal team. He was charged with two counts, one for conspiracy to commit murder, and the second for attempted murder.

He got off with the conspiracy charge. His team tried to argue that he really knew nothing about the two murders, that of Connors and Bourne. In fact, they argued Bourne was not even murdered. He had been diagnosed with COVID-19. That was on the death certificate. It was a weak argument in my view, but it carried the day. I thought the next issue was quite simple. Greene had attempted to murder Berryman and me. I wasn't sure there was much defence to this. But inevitably there was. His legal team argued that he didn't mean to kill us, but was simply trying to scare us. After all, he knew his gun was carrying blanks. That was complete bullshit and I think everybody realized it.

Greene was very glib on the witness stand. He was immaculately dressed and wore his wig. He would attempt to flirt with most of the females in court, including a couple in the jury box. The sort of guy who could sell you a mining license on the moon. In the end, he got off with a lesser charge. He was sentenced to four years with two years suspended. This meant that he would only serve about fourteen months. Inevitably, it would be in an open prison.

Then there was the issue of his malfeasance as it related to stock trading. The evidence was compelling and there was no way he could avoid the punishment. He was banned from trading for five years. In reality, this was a slap on the wrist. He would simply get somebody else to do his trading. He had done this before with no consequences. It was not long before he was promoting another stock, this time a gold exploration company in British Columbia. A lot of trading seemed to be coming from offshore companies, almost certainly his.

This left the issue of what would happen to MMC and Radishon. They had even more highly-priced lawyers than Greene. They had to pay a big fine, but they had done this several times before. For MMC, it was simply the price of doing business. They even found a new use for their drug in the treatment of renal disease. The company had come out of this relatively unscathed, with one exception. They were inevitably sued by the relatives of those who had died. Even this was diluted a bit because they still argued that several of the deaths were a result of suicides as well as pre-existing conditions. There were big payments made, but it all depends on what you call big. Fifty thousand to most people is a sizeable sum. To a pharmaceutical company, it is a couple of days interest payments. It's usually not a problem, anyway. You simply increase the price of your drugs and co-opt a few more doctors to recommend your drug and everything is fine. Five years later, nobody remembers.

So, what happened to us, you may ask? We got some positive press for our efforts and it increased our profits, at least statistically. We needed to increase our cash flow because we had two new members of staff, Arnold and Daphne. And we had one individual on family leave, Jen. And we had to update our downtown accommodation. If we're going to hit the big leagues, we would need something other than a tiny office with a toilet that didn't flush. Perhaps we could do with some hot blonde babe sitting at a reception desk. I know that sounds sexist, but everybody else does it.

Let me tell you about Arnold and Daphne. They were a huge addition. They were brilliant and added a real intellectual element to our team, albeit on a part-time basis. I'm not even sure they were bothered about being paid. They were to help us solve several cases in the following years. And then they got married. This meant that we lost our next-door neighbour but gained two friends. Arnold had done it the old-fashioned way. He moved into Daphne's house in Elbow Park. Not the sort of place you would drop into the neighbours for a cup of sugar.

Arnold developed early signs of Parkinson's, but it didn't slow him very much at all. When they got married, Rita and I gave them a unique gift. We bought them the 50 best foreign films with subtitles. We even popped over occasionally to watch them. Rita and I were slowly getting a bit more sophisticated.

Jen eventually gave birth to twins, one male, and the other female. After three months, she insisted on coming back to work. She was a great mom, but Red was just as good as a father. Shared responsibilities are, I suppose, the way it is these days. Red continued with his education, though most of it had to be online. I believe he was doing Indigenous studies. He inevitably did well. It was going to be a race with Jen as to who would get their Master's degree first.

Louie eventually retired early from the police, but he still kept involved with us. He continued to butcher the English language and at one point made the appalling mistake of thinking that he could act. He couldn't. You wouldn't want to act opposite him. There was always the danger of getting splinters. He tried to work as a prompter, but it never quite worked when the actors would have to ask him to repeat himself. He still loved to drink tuica, but his liver had complained a bit and he had to cut back. But we would always use him as a contact and as a friend. And he rarely lost at Scrabble.

Which leaves me and Rita. Things never really changed for us. We never got married. We never seemed to have the time. Rita's health remained much improved, and she even began to exercise regularly.

She almost got me involved. But I eventually resisted the temptation. I didn't like to sweat. So, we continued to focus on our work. One thing we did was to learn to cook. It was something we did together. I was rehabilitated. I stopped eating takeout junk food. I started to make it myself.

Oops, I forgot one important member of the family. Artie the grey parrot. I couldn't leave him out. And he wouldn't be left out. He needed all the attention in the world, and he talked too much. As Rita said, "He's almost as bad as you, Sid." A couple of months later, I found out why he needed the attention. We had taken him to the vet one day and found out that he was not a him. I thought that explained a lot. Artie was a female. And then it happened. We had always hoped it wouldn't, but it did. He learned a new word 'pizda' from Louie and wouldn't stop saying it. Don't look this word up. We squirt him with water when he says it. Sadly, it hasn't worked yet.

When I look back, I realize that cases such as the present one simply do not come around too often and for a time we had to rely on issues such as "I think my husband is screwing his secretary" and " We seem to be leaking money, but I don't know where." But cases like this paid the bills. In fact, we were doing rather nicely financially, but we were getting into a bit of a rut. We needed a bit of excitement and then one day we got an urgent call. There had been a fatality at the latest professional wrestling show. There was something very unusual about the whole thing. It all looked suspicious though to be fair, so did most professional wrestling, in my opinion. Could we help investigate to find out what had happened and why? And who did the call come from? None other than big Dave Jessop or Igor Ballsorf as the fans knew him. Now, what could Big Dave have to tell us? I picked up the phone to find out. I thought he should join our team.

ABOUT THE AUTHOR

DR. ALAN LEBOEUF was born in an industrial city in the north of England and is still proud to call himself a Salfordian. After 18 years he left home for the last time graduating at Sheffield University, Birmingham University and Trinity College, Dublin. Armed with a Ph.D in Clinical Psychology he moved to Bermuda for seven years as a practicing clinician before moving to his present location in Calgary, Alberta where he continued as a psychologist. Apart from his work as a psychologist, he became a correspondent on a local radio show for CBC and also submitted several papers to academic journals. Nine years later he entered the field of theatre taking the lead in a drama with a local community theatre group and then trapped by the acting bug he appeared in 30 plays over the next few years. He wrote his first play in 2012 and since then has written 19 plays, seven of which have been performed. It was 2019 when he bumped into the mythical character of Sidney Arbuckle and this has led to eight books about this character the second of which you see today.

He has now retired as a clinical psychologist but intends to continue to write until the last page. He continues to support various charities and is still passionate about his favourite pastimes. Cricket and rugby.

Alan hopes you enjoy his work. Feel free to contact him at :
dralan.leboeuf@gmail.com.

Thank you for completing *Frozen in Fear*.

We would love if you could help by posting a review at your book retailer and on the PageMaster Publishing site. It only takes a minute and it would really help others by giving them an idea of your experience.

Thanks

PM Store Author's QR Code
https://pagemasterpublishing.ca/by/Alan-LeBoeuf/

To order more copies of this book, find books by other Canadian authors, or make inquiries about publishing your own book, contact PageMaster at:

PageMaster Publication Services Inc.
11340-120 Street, Edmonton, AB T5G 0W5
books@pagemaster.ca
780-425-9303

catalogue and e-commerce store
PageMasterPublishing.ca/Shop

www.ingramcontent.com/pod-product-compliance
Lightning Source LLC
Chambersburg PA
CBHW070024260626
47159CB00005B/1943